WHITE LITTLE LIES

SARA C. ROETHLE

1

CRISPIN GRIPPED MY ARMS, steadying me. His fresh scent, like the first new leaves of spring, filled my senses. "Easy now, you didn't make it too far this time."

I took a deep breath, willing the dizziness to subside. He was right. We were still in his tower, sparkling sunlight cutting a long line across the floor through a stained glass window. Stacks of books teetered haphazardly around us.

"There, that's better." Crispin released me, then turned back toward his workstation to scribble a few notes.

I watched his broad shoulders, clad in a periwinkle button up, as he continued writing. On anyone else, the color would have been too much. But on him it just sort of... worked. The plaid pants and dapper suspenders probably helped.

One of these days I was going to get a peek at that

journal and see that he was just scribbling *Eva is a failure* over and over again. He was doing his best to help me learn how to travel to the near realms to find my mom, but so far I hadn't managed to go far. The only time I had made it anywhere impressive had been to save him, and that was because he had already forged the pathway. I had something to focus on to get there.

I glanced at Sebastian, leaning against the wall near the window, watching us with a bored expression. He was dressed in his usual black and white, the creases in his trousers as sharp as his cheekbones.

Scowling, I put my hands on my hips. "You may as well leave if you're just going to stand there like that."

"It's only been a week since an elf tried to kill you, and you would like me to leave you unprotected in Emerald Heights?" A flash of fire in his eyes emphasized his words.

I frowned. "Zenith is rotting in a dungeon somewhere. No one else wants to kill me."

"You're being naïve."

Shaking my head, I turned back toward Crispin. His blond hair was mussed from raking his fingers through it so many times, and his blue eyes were weary. I seemed to have that effect on people. At least lately.

He set his journal aside. "I hate to agree with the devil, but there is no sense in throwing caution to the wind. I myself did not exactly enjoy being run off the road by crazed fairies with poisoned blades."

I shifted uncomfortably at his words, remembering

how one of those poisoned blades had pierced Gabriel's chest, which led to me to think of what had happened after that. Waking up in the arms of two different men had been a new experience for me, one we were yet to repeat. One I wasn't sure we *would* repeat if a life wasn't hanging in the balance.

It was also an experience I was avoiding discussing with either of the goblins because my cheeks burned like fire every time I thought of it.

"Earth to Eva." Crispin's intelligent blue eyes sparkled. "Care to share what secret thoughts have you blushing in the middle of our lesson?"

I cringed. "Nothing important. Now let's try again."

Crispin sighed. "As fun as it is having to find you when you shift to an unfamiliar area of the palace, I think we should perhaps call it for the day. I'll try to come up with something else for next time."

I gave him a wary look, and he lifted his hands. "No forging my own paths, I promise. Nearly getting trapped in that tiny room last time was enough to scare me straight." He lowered his voice to a whisper, though Sebastian would hear him regardless. "Not that I minded the *rescuing*."

My entire face heated. The make-out with Crispin was *also* a one time thing. I had only done it to save him. With both Mistral and Gabriel, and hells, sometimes Sebastian, my dance card was more than full.

My eyes flicked toward the devil in question and he smiled at me like he knew exactly what I was thinking.

We had only kissed a handful of times, and each time I boldly declared to myself that it would be the last. But would it? My magic reacted differently to him than it did to the others, and each kiss always left me wanting more, even though I wanted to punch him just as badly.

"And now you have that same look for Sebastian. Curious." I turned to see Crispin stroking his chin.

"Not curious," I grumbled. "Annoying."

Crispin lifted a brow, but didn't comment further. "Elena asked if she could escort you to the border today. I promised I wouldn't tell her father, though gods help me if he finds out."

I rolled my eyes. "She can gallivant around the city shooting people with arrows, but she gets drunk one time and that's what her father is hung up on?"

Crispin shrugged. "I think it was the getting drunk with *werewolves* part that has him on edge."

I pinched my brow and shook my head. Perhaps it had not been my wisest plan bringing everyone to Willowvale, but it had worked out okay in the end. Save for Braxton's cousin Warrick pestering me for Elena's number. I had told him that I wasn't sure if elves even used phones, but that was yet to dissuade him.

My head whipped up as Sebastian suddenly appeared right beside me, instead of leaning against the wall. Since there was no telltale flash of darkness, he had probably just walked over. Man, I was exhausted. Shifting uselessly around the palace could really take it out of a girl.

He offered me his arm, and I narrowed my eyes at him.

"You're going to fall down the stairs if you try to walk on your own."

My eyes narrowed further, but he was right. I was dead on my feet. I took his arm, trying to not delight at the little thrill of dark magic prickling up my skin, instantly tightening things lower.

By the gods, I really needed to find the Realm Breaker to fulfill our contract and get me away from him.

Considering he was a devil, my very soul might hang in the balance.

❯ ❅ ❆ ❅ ❆ ❅ ❆ ❮

"So LISTEN," Elena said as we rode our bucks toward the gates. "I've been thinking about the fairy who cast the glamour to fake your death."

My eyes whipped from our green surroundings to study her face. Part of Sebastian's new contract with Elena's father was to share whatever information either of them had on my mother. Even though Sebastian had garnered that information from *spying* on me, it was technically necessary to share it. Since it would come out anyways, I had told Elena about it too.

"You want to go to the Crystal Vale, don't you?" I smoothed my hands across my buck's fur. At least I was finally trusted to ride on my own after the past week visiting Crispin.

She rolled her eyes toward me. "Well *I* can't go there."

"Only Eva can go there," Sebastian said from my other side. "And it's far too dangerous."

"Those fairies only tried to kill her because they believed Ivan was paying them!" Elena argued.

Sebastian took a deep breath and let it out slowly. "There are many others in the city who still want Eva, and the fairies have made it obvious they will work for the highest bidder." His buck shook its head, unsettled by his irritation.

"It *is* the best lead we have on my mom," I interrupted. "The glamour was aimed specifically at her. Whoever cast it would have needed to know her."

"And what makes you think they're still alive?"

I shrugged. "Until recently, my mom still thought I was dead."

"That does not mean the glamour is still active, only that she stopped looking."

My shoulders hunched against the sun heating my back. "It's still our best lead," I muttered. "Either that, or Lucas."

Sebastian had claimed Lucas was just following orders, that he had no true contact with my mother, but was fulfilling an old debt. Even if it was true, it had to be some debt for the effort he'd put in, not only killing night runners, but harassing me, and even threatening to hold me prisoner in the Silver Quarter.

The latter had convinced me to stay away from him, but I might have to confront him eventually. Even if I could learn to travel to the near realms, I would still need to have a rough idea of where my mother was hiding.

"Just work on your realm jumping," Sebastian said tersely. "Without that, none of the rest of it matters."

Elena chewed her lip like she wanted to say more, but she kept quiet. I had a feeling I would be hearing all about it once Sebastian wasn't around, but that might take a while. The only place I could go to escape him now that the elf king had given him a free pass was the Bogs, and Elena couldn't go there.

And if *I* went there...

I'd had communication with both Gabriel and Mistral since that night, but I hadn't gone long enough to stay within the Citadel. I would have liked to say that maybe I didn't fully trust them, but it wasn't true.

In reality, I just didn't fully trust myself.

2

WE RAN into one of my neighbors on the way up to my apartment. Noel had fairy blood somewhere in her ancestry, but it wasn't strong. Just enough to give her a feel of *otherness* that most wouldn't even notice. She pushed a lock of black hair behind her ear and gave me a coy smile as we passed her on the stairs.

I forced a smile in return. Sebastian had been around so much, I was pretty sure most of the neighbors thought he was my boyfriend. Most of them also wouldn't be able to tell that he was a devil. If they could, they might think a little differently of me.

I glanced at him as we continued toward my door. He seemed oblivious, but I knew it was an act. Sebastian missed very little.

He finally looked down at me as we reached my apartment, but his dark eyes were distant, his thoughts somewhere else. "I will return for you tomorrow."

I could have let it go at just that. I *should* have let it go at just that. But hells, he had saved my life one too many times. It didn't feel right lying to him. "I have a delivery tonight, so if you sense your calling card out and about, that's why."

His eyes were suddenly keen on my face. "You're being foolish."

I lifted a hand to cut him off. "Hey, a girl's gotta eat, and there's nothing in our contract that says I can't take other jobs. But in case you didn't catch the rest of my statement, I will bring my card." It vexed me, but once again, he had saved my cookies one too many times. Every time I'd heard a motorcycle over the past week, I was looking over my shoulder for fae.

"Whatever you will earn for the delivery, I will double it."

I gritted my teeth. "I'm freelance, and this client is a regular. I can't afford to lose them."

He studied me, the sunlight cutting a harsh line across his high cheekbone. "Then I will escort you."

"You don't have to—"

Fire flashed in his eyes. "I have invested far too much time into you to leave you unprotected."

I wrinkled my nose at his words. "Oh, gee, and here I thought you'd actually grown to like me."

"That is an entirely different subject. What time is your delivery?"

I looked at my watch. "I have to leave in two hours."

"Then I will return in two hours." He disappeared in a flash of darkness.

Shaking my head, I reached into my bag for my keys. If Noel had crossed our path just a few minutes later, she would have seen him leaving. I was betting her expression would have been a little different had that been the case.

I unlocked the door and went into my apartment. I had been convincing myself that I was brave enough to go to the Bogs tonight, but with Sebastian hounding me, I might not get the chance. I hated that part of me was relieved. It wasn't like the experience hadn't been wonderful, and I cared deeply about both goblins, but...

I could admit, if only to myself, that dammit, I was embarrassed.

Ringo bounded toward me as soon as I was inside, his blue fur fluffed up with excitement. Sebastian might have a free pass into Emerald Heights, but Ringo was a pure blooded goblin. I was yet to muster the courage to ask King Francis to let him in too.

I crouched down for him to climb into my hands, then lifted him onto my shoulder as I walked toward my bedroom. I was looking forward to two hours of alone time before Sebastian returned.

Well, relatively alone, but I didn't mind Ringo hanging out on my bookshelf.

Braxton popped his head out of his doorway as I passed. His hair was mussed and his eyes groggy, so I must have woken him from a nap. "Just thought you might want to know, there's a giant goblin waiting in your bedroom."

I stopped mid-stride, then took a step back to face Braxton, giving him wide eyes. "How long has he been in there?"

He shrugged. "About an hour."

I winced. "Thanks, I guess."

He gave me a wink. "You two keep it down in there. I need my beauty sleep."

My cheeks burned. I knew it had been a mistake to tell Braxton what happened, but I had to tell *someone*. I had hoped he could give me some advice. Instead, he had laughed his ass off and asked when I had gotten so much cooler than him.

Really, I should have known better.

As Braxton shut his door, I approached my room, my palms already sweating. I turned the knob and went inside, and there Gabriel was, leaning against the wall beside my bed with his arms crossed.

His straight black hair was loose, tucked behind his ears, and his massive arms were mostly bare in his T-shirt. The deep green fabric contrasted beautifully with his brown skin.

"I'm not used to seeing you in regular T-shirts," I said awkwardly, lowering my shoulder so Ringo could hop onto my bed.

I couldn't read Gabriel's expression as he replied, "It's easier to blend in with the humans in the city."

I looked him up and down, all 6'6" of him. "Gabriel, I don't think you blend in *anywhere*."

His expression still unreadable, he pushed away from the wall, straightening to his full height.

"You know, you could have sat on the bed, made yourself comfortable."

"I didn't want to be presumptuous."

I shook my head. "If you say so. So what's up? Why are you here?"

"Mistral believes you are avoiding us. He believes you are embarrassed."

I fought the urge to squirm, turning away to toss my bag onto my bed so he couldn't see my expression. "Not embarrassed, just busy. I was in Emerald Heights all day."

I sensed him stepping toward my back, his nearness and the fact that we were in my bedroom giving me a little thrill.

"Eva—"

I turned toward him abruptly, and he was closer than I had realized. "I'm not avoiding you, I swear." Gods, was it ever lucky that I only had a bargain of truth with Mistral. "It's just that we don't have a lot of time. With things unstable in the Bogs—"

He took my hand, his big fingers swallowing mine up. "If you regret what happened—"

Even just the touch of his hand felt too damn good. "I don't. Seriously, I don't." I took a deep breath, then slowly let it out. Sebastian I could skate around the truth with, but Gabriel... He was just so earnest. It felt wrong. "I've just never dated two people at once, okay?"

His small smile tugged at my heart. For a while, I hadn't even been sure that Gabriel could actually smile. And now, having that smile just for me?

"So we're dating?"

I waved my free hand in the air. "In a vague, nebulous sense of the word."

His smile shifted into a smirk. My opposite hand grew warm in his, my magic rising. He lifted my fingers, my skin gently glowing where it touched his. My magic reacted differently to each of the guys, and the glow mostly seemed to be for him. He leaned down, placing a kiss on my knuckles.

My heart fluttered. "You know, I can't think straight when you do things like that."

He kissed the next knuckle. "Come to the Bogs, Eva."

"I have a delivery tonight."

He turned my hand, extending it to kiss the underside of my wrist.

My breath hitched.

"In how long?" he muttered.

"Two hours."

Another kiss, further up the inside of my arm. "And what do you intend to do until then?"

"Well I was thinking about having some alone time, but suddenly that doesn't sound terribly appealing."

He cradled my arm, kissing the inside of my elbow, leaving a soft glow behind.

I swallowed the lump in my throat, inhaling his earthy, smoky scent. "Mistral didn't send you, did he?"

A flash of a smile again as he lowered my arm and stepped closer. "No, though he is aware I am here."

"And he's totally fine with that?"

He nodded, pushing my hair behind my ear, gazing down at me with heat in his dark eyes.

I saw a flash of blue as Ringo jumped near the door, turning the knob so he could scurry out of the room.

Gabriel cupped my jaw with his large hands and kissed me, tearing away my last shred of resistance. But really, I didn't want to resist. As much as the whole situation made me nervous, I still wanted it. I still wanted both of them.

Gabriel's tongue darted into my mouth and I opened for him, leaning my body against his. He took the invitation to lower his hands to my ass, lifting me so I could wrap my legs around him. The angle was better for both of our necks, and left one of his hands free to skim up my back beneath my shirt, making the rest of my skin ache to be touched in the same way.

He lowered us to the bed, leaning my body back so he could kiss down my neck. As our skin heated, the scent of him filled my nostrils again—earth, ozone, and a hint of woodsmoke. I gripped his chin, bringing his face back to mine for another kiss. His tongue dove into my mouth, his hips grinding against me, letting me feel him through his pants.

He broke the kiss just long enough to remove his shirt, then he reclaimed my lips like he was starving for my touch. The thought of it sent a thrill of pleasure straight to my core. He slipped my shirt upward, removing it much more gently than he had his own. The bra went next, and he took a moment just to look down at me. We had been so consumed with wild goblin magic our first time together, we hadn't had time for all the small stuff, like getting to just enjoy seeing each other naked for the first time.

He lowered his head, sucking one of my breasts into his mouth. I tried to stifle my moan for Braxton's sake, but my magic was really kicking up. I knew once it took over, I would be forgetting all about Braxton and his werewolf hearing.

Gabriel moved to my other breast, sucking it into his mouth, then teasing my nipple with his tongue. As it hardened he gave it an extra little flick, then his hands went under my back, arching it to put me on full display. He grazed my flesh with his teeth, and when I didn't protest, he bit a little harder. I panted, rocking my hips up against him.

His chuckle was a deep rumble against my skin. One hand lowered to unbutton my jeans, then I helped by wiggling my way out of them as he pulled them down. I wrapped my legs back around him in just my panties.

I distantly noted a knock at the front door, but I wasn't expecting anyone. So Braxton could get it. I heard a muffled exchange, then, "Eva! Where are you, darling!"

Gabriel and I both went still, turning our attention to my slightly ajar door.

I heard Braxton's lower voice muttering something.

"Don't worry, I'll rouse her."

My heart pounded in my chest. That was Dawn's voice. And here I was, still clinging half naked to Gabriel. Braxton exchanged pleasantries with my old boss as they approached my door.

"You might want to knock—"

"No look, it's open."

A celestial and a goblin never moved so quickly as Gabriel and I shooting up out of bed, just as my door swung open revealing Dawn with Braxton standing just behind her. At first his face held an apologetic wince, then his hand lifted to cover his silent laughter as soon as he saw what state we were in. Gabriel, shirtless, and me holding his missing shirt over my chest.

A slow smile curved Dawn's red lips. "Well well, Eva, no wonder you never come to see me." She slowly looked Gabriel up and down. "It seems you've found something to keep you *far* too busy."

With my hair mussed and my legs on full display, I pointed toward the living-room. "*Out.*"

Dawn crossed her arms, her emerald pantsuit stretching across her impressive form in a way that only the most expensive, custom-made garment could. "I'll close the door now, but only if you agree to come into the living room and drink the caramel latte I brought you while we have a nice chat."

My cheeks heated. "Fine."

The door shut, and Braxton's laughter became not so silent outside.

Gabriel, seeming entirely unruffled, looked a question at me.

"My old boss." I reached for my jeans, casting a reluctant look at his bare chest, still feeling the urge to lick every inch of his flesh. I quickly darted my eyes away. "She's been keeping an ear out for rumors about the bounty,"

He held out an arm for me to steady myself while I hopped into my jeans. "She's not a night runner."

"No," I agreed. "She's part troll, but mostly human. She runs the agency because she's a good business-woman, not because she knows anything about celestial magic."

I buttoned and zipped my jeans, knowing I needed to go into the living room, but Gabriel was still just standing there, looking scrumptious. "Will you stay for coffee?"

"I usually drink tea."

I huffed. "It's like I don't even know you."

He laughed, wrapping an arm around my waist to pull me close. "Come to the Bogs tonight, Eva."

Heat and magic both coursed through me at the

thought of it, all of the sensation pooling between my legs. "I'll try."

"I can return to escort you to your delivery."

I wrinkled my nose. "Sebastian will be with me. He doesn't want me to get snatched away either."

"Even more reason for me to return." He leaned down, brushing his lips across mine, stealing my breath away.

"Eva, darling! Your coffee is getting cold!"

Still wrapped in Gabriel's arms, I hung my head. "I should go. And don't worry about my delivery. Sebastian may be a pain in the ass, but he has made it clear he has *invested too much time* to lose me. I'll try to come to the Bogs once my job is done."

His expression darkened. "As much as I dislike his presence, I would ask that he escort you to the gates."

Because *that* wouldn't be awkward at all. "Sure," I said, not sure if I would actually go through with it.

He didn't push me further, but the look he gave me made it clear he knew I wasn't being entirely honest. I gave him a quick peck on the cheek, then led the way to the door. He held it open for me, and we both stepped out into the living room.

Dawn perched on one side of the sofa, sipping from a periwinkle colored to-go cup. I knew the location that had those cups, and I never went there because it was way too expensive. A matching cup waited on the coffee table for me.

Braxton had made himself scarce. He tolerated

Dawn, but he had never really liked her. He felt like she took advantage of me. Which was true, but at this point, it was a pretty mutual relationship.

Her eyes lingered on Gabriel as he came to stand beside me.

"I'll see you later," he said, brushing one large hand across the small of my back as he pulled away.

I shivered at the touch, and was angry all over again at Dawn for interrupting us. Although I was at least grateful that she didn't show up any *later*.

We both watched Gabriel walk toward the door and let himself out.

Once he was gone, Dawn chuckled. "I never thought I'd see you in bed with a goblin."

I walked around the coffee table to sit on the other side of the couch. "Personally, I had hoped you would never see me in bed with *anyone*."

"I thought perhaps you were dating an elf, one of the nobility, seeing as how the king's protection now extends to your *roommate*."

She was fishing for information, and I wasn't about to give it to her until the right moment. She would want something in exchange for whatever she had to tell me. I reached for my coffee and took a sip. It was still piping hot. Part of the price tag at *Lapis Brews* was the minor enchantment placed on each cup, keeping the coffee the perfect temperature until the very last drop. The enchantment didn't last forever, but was good for a few hours.

The steamed milk was perfectly creamy and the amount of caramel just right, brightening my mood considerably. I lifted the cup toward her in thanks. "I'm surprised you'd willingly buy coffee from gargoyles."

"I'm willing to go to great lengths for quality, Eva. You know that." She angled her long legs toward me, then leaned back against the sofa cushion. "Now, are you going to tell me what you've been doing in Emerald Heights?"

Ah, it seemed we were jumping straight to the bargaining. I took another slow sip of my coffee, pretending to ponder her question. Finally, I said, "I'm not sure what you mean."

She flashed me a quick smile. "Oh, I do miss you, so I will throw you a nice little crumb." She leaned forward, meeting my eyes steadily. "I believe I have new information on your mother."

My heart fell to my feet.

3

I STARED AT DAWN, my coffee forgotten in my hand. "What did you say?"

She smiled the proverbial crocodile's smile. "Why did King Francis grant you his protection?"

Though my heart was racing, I forced my breathing to slow. My voice came out calm and even. Bully for me. "Why are you so interested in Emerald Heights?"

Her eyes shifted ever so slightly. That was it. She wanted something from the elves.

I leaned back against the sofa cushions, forcing myself to take a sip of my still perfectly hot latte. "Whatever it is you want, I may be able to help you with it." I lifted my free hand, observing my nail beds.

"This stays between us?"

My eyes lifted to her face, which now held an expression I had never seen on her. I was used to the sarcasm, the bartering, the cool calculation... But what I saw now, was hope. My brows lifted. "Of course, as long as this silence goes both ways."

I had thought she just wanted information to sell, and in that case I had to be careful. But I was beginning to doubt my original estimations.

She looked down at the periwinkle cup in her hands, her sleek black bob falling forward on either side of her strong-boned face. "Eva, I'm in love."

I was glad I wasn't drinking my coffee, or else I would have choked on it.

She scowled. "Oh don't look at me like that. I *am* capable of love."

"Could have fooled me," I said before I could help myself.

Her scowl deepened. "Do you want to know what information I have on your mother, or not?"

My mood quickly sobered. "I apologize. You're in love. Please continue."

"His name is Rian. I only met him briefly when he hired a runner, but *gods* Eva, he's perfect."

I bit my tongue, knowing she wouldn't take kindly to me questioning her being in love with someone she had only met once. "Let me guess, he doesn't often leave Emerald Heights?"

"I believe he is nobility, he certainly acted that way, and he spoke like some of the old ones from their far realm."

Well now I was even more curious. "What did he need the agency for?"

"He wanted a package delivered to the Crystal Vale, and a package was acquired for him in return. A bit of a trade with neither party having to meet beyond their boundaries." She waved it off with one hand. "You know how it is."

I did know. Trade was a big part of business for night runners, bringing something beyond a boundary and returning with trade or payment. It wasn't unusual, but... the Crystal Vale? What might an elf need to trade with the fae? And could it possibly have anything to do with the fae the king sent in an attempt to scare me?

"How long ago did you meet him?" I asked.

"It's only been a few weeks. I've done my best to find more information on him, but you know how the elves are."

I thought things over. It would have been a lot more convenient for her to fall in love with a goblin. With her troll blood, she could actually walk across the boundary to the Bogs. But not Emerald Heights. She couldn't step foot there unless she received a direct invitation from the king, like Sebastian.

"I'm going to Emerald Heights tomorrow. I'll ask around." And it wouldn't be just for Dawn. If Rian had just been running an errand for the king or for himself, he was probably harmless. But if he was instead involved with Zenith... Zenith's little brother tried to kill me. I couldn't be too careful.

Dawn's face lit up at my words. "Oh Eva, you're a lifesaver."

"I certainly am. Now about my mother..."

Her normal calculating smile slipped back into place. "Of course. I'll tell you everything I know once you come through on Rian."

"Like hell—" Incensed, I started to stand.

She cut me off with a laugh. "Calm yourself, Eva. I wouldn't do that to you." She lifted her periwinkle cup. "In fact, we even began this meeting with a hint."

I stared at the cup, racking my brain. "My mom has assumed the identity of a barista and is hiding in plain sight?"

She rolled her eyes, lowering the cup. "The gargoyles, Eva. I couldn't find anything on the angelic you mentioned, other than the fact that he's powerful and not to be trifled with, so I went for the next best thing."

I blinked at her. It was actually pretty clever. The angelics would never talk—all of their gossip was firmly locked away in the Silver Quarter. But the gargoyles... Despite their difference in appearance, they were actually from the same realm. Another near realm, though most had lost the power to travel there. While it was rare to see a gargoyle actually associating with an angelic, they could cross the border to the Silver Quarter, and many lived beyond the iridescent gates. If anyone wanted information on an angelic, a gargoyle was a pretty good place to start.

"What did you learn?" I asked as my thoughts finally caught up with me.

She looked smug for a moment, and I was about to yell at her, then she answered, "I learned that about a month ago, Lucas received a message. No one knows what it said, but he's hardly been around the Silver Quarter since. Many believe he's on some sort of top-secret mission."

I deflated with every word. I pretty much knew all of this. Lucas owed my mom a favor. He received a message with orders that he would have to complete to repay that favor, and he started stalking night runners after that. But it wasn't some huge secret—he'd told Sebastian about it in an attempt to convince him to release me to Lucas' *care*.

Dawn closely watched my shifting expression. "This is obviously not news to you, and while I would have *appreciated* you sharing with me who killed my last night runner, I'll let it go. The important news is who delivered that message. Not another angelic, not a celestial, but a *devil*."

My eyebrows shot up. Now it made sense why the gargoyles would even care about some secret message. There weren't many devils in the city, and for one to have a secret exchange with an angelic?

"Do you know the devil's name?" I pressed.

Dawn almost seemed embarrassed as she answered, "No, but I'm working on it. All I know is that she appeared female. And as long as you find out all you can about Rian, I will find out all I can about the devil."

I sipped my coffee, deep in thought. If a devil was

the one to deliver my mother's message, did that mean she was hiding in the hells? Though Sebastian was yet to admit it to me, I had learned he couldn't actually go there. He was just as trapped as most everyone else. Had my mom been hiding in his home realm all this time?

If it was true that would mean—

Fear trickled through me. It would mean that once I learned to realm jump, I would need to go to the hells. And if Sebastian's powers were any indication, a realm full of devils was a dangerous place to be.

4

I GRIPPED the strap of my messenger bag, giving Ringo a reassuring light pat as I walked down the street toward the bus stop, comfortable in my jeans, black T-shirt, brown leather jacket, and brown boots. The night was still a little warm for the hoodie I had on underneath the jacket, but I felt better looking a little more anonymous on the crowded city buses. I could pull my hood forward and pretend no one else existed.

Of course, this time Sebastian would be with me, a thought that made me almost giddy. Sebastian, in his fancy clothes, crammed onto a city bus. I could already picture it, and it was hilarious.

We reached the bus stop and he moved to stand near my shoulder. "You know, you could just shift to your location and I could meet you there."

"Ha *ha*." I rolled my eyes.

"True." He smirked. "You would probably end up in a dumpster."

I huffed, but didn't respond. I was going to get to see him uncomfortable on a city bus. Nothing was going to ruin my good mood.

"We could take a cab. My treat."

"You're the one who insisted on coming. We do things my way." I tugged my jacket straight, glancing over at the covered seating.

A pair of humans sat on one edge of the bench, leaving ample space between themselves and the gargoyle sitting at the other end, her skin solid gray, and as stony as her expression. She wore a long-sleeve shirt altered to accommodate her massive, batlike wings. They looked like they were made out of stone, but could move just as nimbly as a bird's.

For the hundredth time, I thought over what Dawn had told me. Whatever gargoyle had been involved had surely just been a witness, but the female devil? Hell, Sebastian might even know her. It would be stupid of me to not ask him, but it was my natural reflex to not share all information with him, even after everything we'd been through.

"What are you thinking?" Sebastian's deep voice startled me out of my thoughts.

"Who says I'm thinking anything?"

"You get a little dent right there." He prodded the space between my brows with his fingertip.

I swatted his hand away. "I do not."

The bus arrived, already packed. It was totally neutral ground within the city, and I could see every type of person within. Goblins in leather jackets with their hair spiked, elves looking like they had just stepped out of the school library, and everything in between. But most of them would have human blood. The older, pure-blooded creatures were usually tucked away behind their boundaries, pretending they didn't intermingle with humans.

The doors opened with a hiss, and I led the way up the steel steps, glancing around for a place to fit in. There were no seats, of course, but a few loops hung from the ceiling in the back for standing room only. I hustled to the nearest one, not wanting to hold up the line.

Sebastian shoved himself in at my back, between me and a man who looked more troll than human. The feel of Sebastian's chest against my back made my body go tight, and not in a bad way. His dark magic raised the tiny hairs at the nape of my neck.

He leaned in close, his cheek brushing mine. "You're doing this to punish me." There was something low and suggestive in his tone, totally inappropriate on a crowded bus.

I swallowed the lump in my throat, realizing the fault in my plan. With Sebastian pressed against my back, all I could think of was the feel of his lips on mine, his hands roaming my body. Hells, I was already sleeping with two guys, wasn't that enough?

My magic didn't seem to think so. It kicked up in reaction to his nearness.

His hand found my waist, his cheek moving once more against mine. "You may want to calm yourself, dear Eva."

"Easy for you to say," I muttered.

The bus started moving, pushing my body more firmly against him when he didn't rock back in the slightest. Stars burst inside of me, pooling into liquid heat.

Yeah, definitely too hot for the extra layer of clothing. There was no way I was pulling my hood up now, not with my entire face burning.

"What did your former employer want with you?"

I stiffened at his words. "Do you really have nothing better to do than watch me all the time?"

"Maybe I wouldn't have to watch you if you didn't keep so many secrets." His hand was at my waist again, gripping just a little too tightly.

"I guess I'll have to start spying on you too, considering how much you tell me."

"Touché." His grip loosened, but his hand remained. A light touch, but a *possessive* one.

I had made a good point, but I did want to know about the female devil, and Sebastian was my best path to that information. It would be stupid of me to put all my faith in Dawn. She would definitely try to learn what I needed to know, but as far as I knew, she didn't have access to any actual devils.

I turned my head, trying to put my mouth close to his ear, but with him standing straight again, it was hard to reach with my back to him. I crooked a finger, giving him an expectant look, and he finally leaned forward, folding his body around me.

"A female devil was the one who brought my mom's orders for Lucas."

He tensed, letting me know it was either information he didn't know, or information he didn't want me to know. "What else?"

"That's it. Dawn is going to try to find out more in exchange for me tracking down her crush in Emerald Heights."

He snorted. "A troll with an elf?"

A grunt from the troll behind him signaled that he had spoken a little too loudly, though he didn't seem to care. I guess when you could wield shadows like weapons, you didn't really worry about the size of your opponent.

I shrugged. "It could happen. And she's mostly human," I whispered.

Ringo chose that moment to finally make himself known in my satchel. "Troll enough to eat goblins," his tiny voice hissed.

"She's not going to eat you," I whispered back.

We were starting to draw odd glances. The driver hit the brakes, and my body lurched. Sebastian snaked his arm further around my waist, his palm splayed across my lower belly, and oh gods, who had been the one to think it was a good idea to take the bus?

Oh yeah. Me. Served me right to think I could make a devil uncomfortable. He seemed perfectly content with his arm around my waist, and with a troll glaring at his back.

That was Sebastian. Not a damn care in the world.

At least, as far as any outside observers were concerned. They probably just thought I was his girlfriend, but they couldn't be further from the truth. I knew his possessive attitude had little to do with romantic inclinations, and more to do with our contract. I was *his* night runner, as far as he was concerned, and he wasn't above killing to protect me.

That part wasn't bad. But the rest was annoying. I started walking toward the front of the bus as we approached our stop, then had to grip the railing to keep from falling forward. Sebastian was already at my back again, waiting for me to move.

I glared at him, then hurried toward the door as it opened.

My delivery tonight was simple, and I knew just where to go. I strode confidently down the sidewalk toward the bakery on the corner. It was run by nymphs, a rarity in the city, especially since they didn't have a boundary to keep them safe. But they hadn't come from another realm. They belonged here. At least the here before everything became asphalt and towering buildings.

I glanced through the glass door before entering, finding the small interior nearly vacant. Just a few lingering patrons at the late hour. I stepped inside, recognizing the woman behind the counter.

Seraphina was tall and willowy, her brown skin just a few shades lighter than her wildly wavy hair, currently pulled back into a thick braid. In her true form her skin looked like tree bark, and her large almond eyes held centuries of knowledge.

She started to smile at me as I approached the counter, then her smile faltered when Sebastian stood a little too close.

"You have a new bodyguard now?" I had heard her voice many times before, but it was always deeper than expected, filled with the resonant, rumbling power of the forest. The old bodyguard would have been Braxton. He had come with me a few times on the pretense of watching my back, but really he just wanted the baked goods.

"Something like that."

She glanced past us at her few remaining patrons. "Give me a moment to chase away the stragglers and close up. Then we'll discuss the delivery."

"We'll have two of those while we wait." Sebastian reached around me to tap the glass, pointing at... something. I assumed they were pastries, but they were perfectly round and smooth, and colored a pale green.

There was no accounting for taste.

Seraphina lifted a brow at me, but plated the

pastries and slid them across the counter. "My treat. I won't be long."

Sebastian took our plates, then walked toward a table near the far window.

"I guess we're going over *here*," I muttered sarcastically under my breath, following him.

I slid into the booth across from him, then looked down at the strange pastry. "Do you have any idea what this is?"

"No. Hence my interest."

I lifted my eyes to his face. "It must be nice to live your life entirely based on your whims."

"Says the woman who *adopts* every goblin she comes across. Small, or so very very large."

I glared at him. "Touché."

As Seraphina shooed out her remaining customers, I lifted the green pastry to my mouth and took a bite. It was incredibly soft and fluffy, and tasted like salty seaweed. I wrinkled my nose, then set the pastry back down. "She probably makes those for the water nymphs and merfolk."

Sebastian's eyes danced with amusement, his pastry untouched before him. "I did actually already know that."

My glare deepened. Of course he would trick me into eating a nasty pastry just for fun.

The door clicked behind us as Seraphina escorted out the last of her customers. I heard the lock sliding into place, then she returned to our table.

She crossed her arms, looking down at us, then nodded toward the back room. "Just you."

"Of course."

Sebastian narrowed his eyes at me as I stood.

"Client confidentiality," I explained.

He still didn't seem satisfied, but he didn't interfere as I followed Seraphina into the back. Maybe he was wondering if I would slip out the rear exit. It wouldn't do me any good unless I tossed his card into the trash, but I knew he didn't think highly of my reasoning skills. So he probably wouldn't put it past me.

The door shut behind us as Seraphina walked past metal shelves of baking supplies toward an impressive array of whisks and spoons.

She turned back toward me, arms still crossed. "How could you bring someone else on your delivery? You know how sensitive the situation is. Braxton is one thing, but this?" She waved a hand toward the door. "A total stranger?"

I lifted a brow. "Do I? You still have never told me what I'm delivering to your sister every other month. And I've been making deliveries for you since I worked back at the agency."

She pursed her lips. "Yes, but no one can know that I'm sending things to her at all. I have been disowned by my family. I won't have the same thing happen to her."

I opened my mouth to say Sebastian wouldn't tell anyone, but did I know that for sure? Maybe someday he would have a reason to blackmail Seraphina, and I would have given him exactly what he needed. "I'm sorry. I didn't think it through. He's been helping me with some stuff, and he just wanted to come to watch my back."

She tilted her head, studying me. "Something about your words is not entirely true."

Oh the joys of dealing with magical creatures. Sometimes they could sense lies, or even half-truths, but you never knew which ones would have the skill.

"It's all true," I sighed. "I just left out the part where he's a devil and I have a contract with him. That's why you're sensing that I'm nervous." I didn't really owe her an explanation, but she was an old client, and an easy delivery. I didn't want to lose her.

Her eyes flew wide. "You brought a *devil* on my delivery?"

"You couldn't tell what he was?"

"How could I?" She seemed offended. "They hide what they are very well until they want you to know."

Funny, because I had figured out what Sebastian was pretty quickly. Of course, he had used his powers on me from the start. Bastard.

"Do you want me to come back for the delivery tomorrow?"

Her eyes flicked toward the closed door. "No," she breathed. "It has to be tonight." She met my gaze. "You have a contract with him. Can you not add an addendum?"

I wrinkled my brow. "You mean like add a clause that he can't tell anyone about tonight?"

She nodded sharply.

I winced. "Maybe, technically, but he never agrees to things for free."

"You are the one who brought him here."

"Right, right," I muttered. "I'll take care of it."

She had already turned away, reaching for a small brown package on the counter. She held my gaze as she handed it to me. "Don't make me regret this, Eva."

I took the package. "I promise I won't." Of course, with how she had reacted to Sebastian, I would just not mention the small goblin in my satchel. I didn't think *he* would ever be coming back to blackmail her.

Not wanting to disturb him, I braced the package under my arm. "I'll see you the month after next?"

She hesitated, then finally nodded. "*Alone* next time."

"Of course. Bye, Seraphina."

She crossed her arms to watch me go. "Bye, Eva. And get yourself away from that devil as soon as possible."

I waved my hand back at her as I went for the door. "Trust me, that's been the plan from the start."

Unfortunately I didn't think that would be happening any time soon. But Seraphina didn't need to know that.

Sebastian was already standing when I reached our table. "Is everything well?"

"Well enough," I grumbled. "But we need to have a chat on the way."

He followed me toward the door, and something told me he already knew what the chat would be about. And he was quite pleased with it.

)))●●●●●(((

"It's not wise to involve yourself in the affairs of nymphs."

I glanced back at Sebastian, the package now secure in my satchel with Ringo. I had told him that Seraphina's situation was complicated, and required secrecy. "You know that's what they say about devils."

Safe on the sidewalk, I peered at the headlights of oncoming traffic, wondering what the chances were of catching a cab. I always delivered Seraphina's packages to the Lower City Lake, never actually seeing the recipient. Normally I would take a bus, but I really wasn't thrilled with the idea of doing that again with Sebastian.

"Where are you to take the package?" he asked, apparently not able to read my thoughts after all, though sometimes it seemed like he could.

I glanced over my shoulder at him. "Yeah, about that. I'm going to need your solemn vow that you will speak of this to no one."

He lifted a dark brow. "My solemn vow?"

Gods, why had I even agreed to this? She was just

one client. I should have told her to shove her package where the sun don't shine.

But I was a professional. And I had a reputation to uphold. "I need the promise added to our contract," I grumbled.

I hated his smug smile. "In exchange for what?"

I crossed my arms, turning toward him, stepping out of the way as a couple of loud teenagers barreled past us. "You're the one who insisted on coming with me, now you're risking me my client. Can't you just add it in?"

He leaned toward me, shortening himself to put us at eye level. "Now where is the fun in that?"

"It's not about fun," I snapped. "This job is important to me. I won't let you endanger my client."

His dark magic prickled up my skin as he smiled. "I will add it into the contract."

My shoulders slumped with relief. "Great—

"If you agree to keep my card on you at *all* times. No more leaving it behind. Not even when you go to the Bogs."

I clenched my hands into fists. "That is *so* not an even trade."

"I only want to keep you safe, dear Eva."

"Only so no one else can use me instead of you."

He lifted one shoulder in a graceful half shrug. "Carry your card at all times, and I will swear a vow of secrecy for not only this client, but all clients. As long as our contract is in play, I will protect you at further deliveries at no additional cost."

I wanted to argue that he wouldn't be coming on any more deliveries, but I knew it probably wasn't the truth. Until we figured out the mystery surrounding my mother, people would want to kidnap me, or worse. And I still hadn't fully gotten over the feeling of having a blade at my throat, knowing my death was only seconds away.

I held out my hand, though I maintained my glare.

He wrapped his long fingers around my palm, gripping far too tightly. His dark magic wrapped around us, and I knew the new contract was sealed.

I continued glaring at him. "You're the worst."

Still gripping my hand, he leaned his face right in front of mine, close enough to kiss. "You don't really think that, dear Eva."

"Go to hell."

He laughed, releasing my hand. He walked past me, back in the direction of the bus stop.

I hurried after him. "We can take a cab this time."

"Oh no." He strolled along with his hands in his pockets, shoulders back, city lights reflecting off his black hair. "I found the bus rather enjoyable."

The card in my back pocket felt heavier already.

5

THE COOL AIR skimming across the top of the lake hit my face with a wash of fertile scents—rich soil, algae, and a hint of magic. Rumor had it that some of the things swimming in the depths of the Lower City Lake were beyond the imagination. Not just naiads, but ancient creatures entirely lost to myth.

I personally thought it was all a load of crap. Naiads loved the water just as much as they loved playing tricks on anyone who came too close to it.

Luckily, we weren't going to be diving below the depths tonight. I looked around the dark forested park. There had been a few people lingering near the borders, but fewer still would brave the deeper parts of the massive park at night.

Ringo clung to my shoulder, pressing against my neck beneath my hair. I could feel him trembling slightly.

"Don't worry," I soothed. "Nothing will be able to snatch us." Maybe I wasn't big and scary, but I was great at escaping when people tried to grab me.

Sebastian appeared suddenly at my shoulder, making me jump. "No one is here."

"I know. I leave the package in a different place around the park every time. I'm just trying to find where I'm supposed to leave it now."

I could feel the warmth of him near my back as he asked, "And why is it taking you so long to find the location?"

I glowered. "We're delivering a package to a nymph. She makes a single flower grow where she wants me to leave it, and her magic disguises it once I put it down."

"And why all of the secrecy?"

I turned toward him, putting my hands on my hips. "Why all of the questions?"

He lowered his chin. "I swore your little vow. You need not protect the nymph from me."

I rolled my eyes. He was right, which meant his questions were just actual curiosity. And it *was* a strange delivery. Every other month, Seraphina would send a package to her sister. Whatever was within was important enough to risk her sister being disowned, just like she had. And it wasn't as simple as just being cut off from their family. They would also be cut off from the magical well each family possessed.

I started walking the perimeter of the lake, looking

for the small white flower. "I don't know what's in the package, so I don't know why it's so important."

He appeared right at my side again, then walked along with me. "You mean you've never taken a peek?"

"Not my business."

"You are a very strange sort of human."

"So I've been told."

We kept walking, only the sound if night insects, occasional splashes in the water, and the distant sound of traffic to accompany our footsteps. It was almost peaceful, and I missed being out in nature. There were plenty of pockets of it within the city, the spaces nurtured by creatures who would quite literally die without it. Many of them had been around before the city rose up around them, and they would remain long after it crumbled to dust.

I stopped walking. "Did you hear that?"

Sebastian gave me a bored look. "You mean the woman crying behind that bush over there?"

I gave him an affronted look, then hurried toward the bush in question. The cry had been light and stifled, like she was trying to hide the sound, but it was there. The bush rustled as I neared it, then a woman dove out, trying to run, but she stumbled and crashed hard into the ground, her legs tangling in her long white dress.

"We're not going to hurt you," I soothed, cautiously approaching as her body heaved with heavy sobs. Long black hair hid her face from view. It was hard to tell in the moonlight, but I thought her visible skin might have held a bluish tinge.

She tried to brace herself up with her thin, bony arms, then fell back to the ground. She was clearly hurt, though I couldn't see the injuries. The hem of her long dress was stained with mud.

"Just go," she sobbed. "I deserve my fate."

I took another cautious step toward her. Sebastian had disappeared at some point—probably looking for what had injured her. Or *who*. There really was no telling this deep in the park.

Ringo's fur tickled my ear. "She smells wrong," he whispered.

His words made my slow steps falter. I had walked into one too many traps lately to not be cautious. "Can you tell me what hurt you?"

She managed to push her hair back out of her face enough to look at me. Her features were striking, and highly recognizable. A wide mouth and big almond eyes, blue instead of brown. "You're the night runner. You know my sister."

Okay so not a trap. Probably. I slowly knelt beside her so she wouldn't have to turn to look up at me. "You're Seraphina's sister?"

She started to nod, but winced. "I came here to tell you to stop bringing the packages. But I was stupid. They saw me and they—"

A twig snapped somewhere nearby. I glanced

around at our dark surroundings, but there was no sign of Sebastian, or whoever had hurt the nymph.

"Who's *they*?" I kept my eyes lifted, searching for signs of danger.

"I don't know," she rasped. "But I think they've been following me. I didn't want to lead them to my sister, so I was going to tell you to stay away. But they found me." She lightly shook her head. "I was so sure I hadn't been seen."

Sebastian appeared beside me and I had to stifle a scream.

The girl—whose name Seraphina had never given— looked at him with raw, wide-eyed horror.

"He's with me," I soothed over the pounding of my heart, shaking my head at the infuriating devil.

"There is no one else around, save the goblin who followed us here."

It was my turn for wide-eyed horror. "We were followed?"

One of his shoulders bobbed. "I assumed you had noticed. She's not far. She believes she is still hidden."

I swiped a palm across my face, shaking my head. Gabriel must have told Mistral about the delivery. But I would deal with that later.

"Come on," I said to the girl. "We need to get you out of here. Do you think you can stand?"

She hesitated, her eyes darting between us, then she hung her head almost touching the ground. "I cannot."

I looked at Sebastian expectantly.

"You mean to take her with us?" His tone let me know how utterly ridiculous he thought the idea was.

"She's hurt. Of course we're going take her with us."

The look he gave me could have turned even a vampire to stone. "What do you intend to do with her? Bring her to your home? Further endanger your roommate?"

I knew he didn't care about Braxton, but he made a good point. "We'll take her to her family."

"No!" she gasped. "They cannot know I was here. Just leave me. I'll make it back on my own."

"We're not leaving you," I said patiently. "We'll take you to a hospital." I still hadn't even seen her injuries, and couldn't quite tell what was wrong with her. But she was definitely in pain.

"A human doctor would not know how to treat a nymph," Sebastian said caustically.

He was probably right. Most of the more magical creatures tended to take care of their own. Their anatomy was just too different from that of a human. Even werewolves usually had their own doctors.

Kneeling next to the nymph, I continued looking at Sebastian, waiting for him to make a helpful suggestion. Nymphs didn't have elven or goblin blood, so Emerald Heights and the Bogs were both out of the question, unless we wanted to wake King Francis in the middle of the night and ask him for a pass.

I doubted that that would go over well.

Sebastian looked like he tasted something sour. "You're not going to let this go, are you?"

"You're speaking to the girl who now has a goblin companion just because trolls were trying to eat him."

He scowled at the blue creature in question. "Fine, but next time you're being stubborn about something, *don't*."

I lifted one hand in a salute. "I will be the most agreeable little celestial you ever did meet."

With an irritated huff, Sebastian knelt down, then lifted the nymph into his arms like she weighed nothing.

She hissed in pain, but I still didn't see any wounds. "Why are you doing this?"

"Because you're hurt and you need help," I said simply.

"Can we get on with this?" Sebastian didn't so much as glance at the woman in his arms.

I gestured toward the distant city lights. "Lead the way."

He did. And with the nymph in his arms, he couldn't dart around in his ominous shadows. He couldn't travel that way with another person, though he had only admitted it once during an emergency. He wasn't as all powerful as he seemed.

Well, he was still pretty scary, he just couldn't dart around with another person, and he couldn't return to the hells. Eventually that secret information would actually do me some good.

Even if that good was just the opportunity to piss him off precisely the right time.

It would totally be worth it.

6

WE HAD LEARNED that the nymph's name was Aaliyah, just before she lost consciousness. I walked slightly ahead of Sebastian, following his directions, keeping lookout for anyone who might ask questions about the unconscious woman in his arms. We had taken a maze of back alleys where any denizens knew to mind their own business, but occasionally we had to step out into the light.

Where we were going was anyone's guess, but I knew Sebastian had connections. He was far more capable of finding help for Aaliyah than I was.

I noticed out the corner of my eye as he stopped abruptly.

I glanced around, wondering if we had reached our destination, but all I could see was a dirty alleyway and a few dimly lit windows high above us. "You better not be planning on tossing her in a dumpster," I whispered.

He lowered his chin, his annoyance clear, then he tipped his head back, gesturing toward the stretch of alley behind us.

"What? I asked, flinging out my hands, feeling tired and annoyed myself.

He sighed heavily, gesturing once more with his eyes that there was something behind us.

With a huff, I marched past him back down the alley. I wasn't really looking for anything, so I nearly screamed when I walked past a woman crouching behind a pile of discarded boxes.

"What the hell!"

Gladiola lifted her purple tinted palms. "I'm sorry, I'm sorry. I was trying to keep my distance, but these alleys are like a maze. I didn't want to lose you."

I crossed my arms as the goblin woman stood to her full height, which was about my height. "And why are you attempting to not *lose* me?" I held up a hand. "Wait. Don't even bother answering that. Gabriel told Mistral about my delivery. You all need to stop worrying so much." I cast a meaningful look back at Sebastian as I said it, but he only watched us blandly, the nymph still cradled in his arms.

Gladiola straightened her silvery hair, then tugged the collar of her black coat up around her neck. "Hey, I'm not worried. I'm just following orders."

My annoyance quickly faded as I realized something. "You were at the park. Did you see what hurt her?" I held a hand back toward Aaliyah as Sebastian moved closer.

Gladiola's brow furrowed. "No. I was on the bus with you, and got off each time you did."

My eyes narrowed. "You weren't on that bus. I would have noticed you."

She lifted a brow. "Honey, you weren't noticing much of anything with *that one* putting his hands on you and whispering in your ear." She nodded toward Sebastian.

Was that a hint of accusation in her tone? "Whatever," I grumbled. "You did your job, now you can leave. The nymph is injured and we need to take care of her."

"My job is to make sure nothing happens to *you*." She squared her shoulders. "I'm not leaving."

"Let her come," Sebastian sighed.

I balked at him. "Seriously? You're going to cooperate with a goblin?"

He wrinkled his nose as his eyes lowered to the nymph in his arms. "I for one do not plan on caring for this woman myself. It will surely take more than the remainder of the night, and *you're* busy tomorrow." He gave me a pointed look.

"I'm sure Crispin will understand if we have to postpone."

"We have wasted enough time." He turned away with the nymph in his arms and started walking.

I wasn't sure if he meant we had wasted enough

time tonight, or wasted enough time not finding my mother, but at the moment, it didn't really matter.

I shrugged at Gladiola. "Let's go, I guess."

"How do you stand him?" she whispered.

"I heard that." His voice echoed from around the next bend.

Gladiola flinched. "You don't think he's gonna curse me, do you?"

I started walking. "Devils don't curse you. They just trick you into infernal contracts and then they annoy you for all of eternity."

"Duly noted." She caught up to walk at my side, our steps echoing around the narrow alley. "So what's the deal with the nymph? Why are we helping her?"

"She's a client's sister. Hopefully we'll find out the rest when she regains consciousness." I glanced at her. "So why were you sent instead of Gabriel?"

"Because Gabriel didn't want to piss you off, and it was agreed that you wouldn't be mad at just little old me." She waggled her eyebrows at me.

I rolled my eyes as we turned in the directions Sebastian had gone. She was right, of course, but I wouldn't say so out loud. "I wouldn't have thought they would worry so much about it."

"We all worry, Eva." Her tone sobered considerably. "We all know what happened at Evenlee, and what hangs in the balance. You're the best hope my people have."

I blanched at her words, my steps faltering. "You *all*

know?" As in they *all* knew I'd had sex with Mistral out in the open to help him control wild goblin magic before it could swallow a village—

"Your face right now," she laughed. "It is so very clear you were raised amongst humans. Goblins are not so rigid about such things."

"Yeah, I'm beginning to realize that." Like how Mistral didn't mind at all that I was also sleeping with his closest friend. And how he didn't seem to mind that I had kissed both Crispin and Sebastian. Well, the latter he minded only because he hated the devil in question.

We took another turn to find Sebastian waiting for us.

"Do I even want to ask what you're thinking right now?" Gladiola whispered, studying my expression.

"It's complicated," I muttered.

She turned her attention to the devil watching us impatiently. "Yeah, I don't doubt that. Not in the slightest."

"If you're both through," Sebastian said tersely. "We have arrived."

I glanced at the solid brick walls on either side of us. "We have arrived where?"

"At one of my dwellings." He turned toward the nearest wall, shifting his grip on Aaliyah to wave one palm in front of the bricks. Shadows swarmed across the wall, and when they cleared, there was a door.

I walked toward it, my jaw hanging open. The door was ornately carved dark wood, completely out of place amongst the stained bricks and nearby city sounds. "*That* was not there a minute ago."

"How astute of you. Now if you would open it, I would greatly like to disencumber myself."

I looked at the unconscious nymph, then back at the door. "Disencumber yourself. Sure." I turned the doorknob, at first only seeing darkness, then warm light filled the narrow hallway.

Sebastian walked past me, momentarily cutting off my view. "Shut the door after you come in. It will disguise itself once more."

Gladiola stepped up beside me. "We don't have anything like *that* in the Bogs."

"No you just have trolls, magical lighting, and women living underwater in your rivers."

"Ooh, don't tell me you met a merrow." She stepped cautiously into the hallway. Sebastian had already gone up a wide set of wooden stairs.

"If merrows like to grab humans by their hair and drag them underwater, then yes." I followed her inside, shutting the door behind me. I watched it for a moment to see if it would disappear, but nothing happened. Maybe it only disguised itself from the outside.

"Yep. That's basically what they do." She walked down the hallway, her head turning back back-and-forth as yellow lights behind glass sconces increased their glow with our passing.

She reached the wooden stairs Sebastian had gone up, then stopped. "I think I'll let *you* take the lead here."

I snorted, stepping around her to go up the stairs. "Aren't you supposed to be protecting me?"

She followed me up. "Yeah, but who's going to protect *me*? You have a contract to keep you safe."

I reached the top of the stairs, then stood rooted to the spot, looking around a posh penthouse. One wall was all windows, but the view was too high. We had only gone up one set of stairs, but it seemed like we were twenty stories up.

Sebastian was at the other end of the open floor plan, beyond a gleaming chrome kitchen with white marble countertops. He had set Aaliyah on a fluffy white couch that looked soft as a cloud. It nearly swallowed her up.

"*Dude.*" I walked past the kitchen, looking around at the rest of the furnishings. Dark wood with simple lines and more plush white furniture. "I have so many questions. But first, is that view real?" I pointed to the city lights that looked twenty stories down.

Sebastian gave me a bored look. "It is. Apartments like this are not uncommon. They are fabricated by the fairies."

Gladiola had kept pace with me to stand close to my shoulder, as if she really did expect me to protect her. "So the stairs were the illusion, not the view?"

"Indeed." He looked down at the nymph. "Whatever you intend to do with her, I suggest you do it soon. Her heartbeat has begun to slow."

My eyes flew wide. "Why didn't you say something

sooner!" I fell to my knees beside the sofa, then felt Aaliyah's pulse. It was slow like Sebastian claimed, but still there.

"Where are her injuries?" Gladiola asked.

I looked her over, but I couldn't see anything externally wrong. "I don't know. She lost consciousness before she could tell us what happened. She said someone was after her—" I shook my head, thinking back. "She couldn't stand on her own. She could barely even sit up."

Gladiola nodded along with my words. "Unless she has some sort of other internal damage, my guess would be poison. Something to slow the heart, make the organs shut down."

I shuddered at her words, looking down at Aaliyah. She was already paler than when we first found her, save some light bruising beneath her eyes. "But she said someone was after her. What did they do, catch her and pour poison down her throat? Why not just kill her?"

Gladiola pushed Aaliyah's hair out of her face, her brow furrowed. "All good questions, but we won't get any answers unless we can reverse what's happening to her."

Completely out of my depth, I looked over at Sebastian.

Fire flashed in his dark eyes, making Gladiola gasp. "I suppose you expect *me* to somehow fix this for you?"

I didn't know what to say. It was ridiculous asking a devil for help. But... he'd helped me before.

"It is a waste of time."

I glared at him. "It's not a waste of time. She could *die*."

"You do not even know her."

I stood, facing him. "That's not any reason to let her die."

We stood staring at each other, at an impasse.

I crossed my arms, maintaining my glare.

"Don't even try threatening me with your silly time-lines again. I know you won't really delay in anything. Not after all you've learned."

He was being vague in front of Gladiola, but he had a point. Now that I knew what my mom had gone through, and why she was being chased, I was intent on finding out who was chasing her. I was going to find her, and fix the mess she had inadvertently made of my life. But that left me with nothing to hold over Sebastian's head.

"Please don't let her die."

He narrowed his eyes at me. "You're begging me now? I would have thought you too prideful."

Sensing an opening, I got down on my knees and grabbed one of his hands before he could pull it away. "Please Sebastian, please don't let the nymph die?" I gave him my best puppy dog eyes.

"You're being ridiculous."

I held tight to his hand, doing my best impression of a puppy dog whimper.

"Stop that."

I whimpered louder, edging closer, still gripping his hand.

"You are absolutely infuriating."

I wanted to say, *Right back at ya*, but I wasn't about to let my groveling be in vain, so instead I whimpered even louder.

"Fine," he sighed, rolling his eyes skyward. "But you're coming with me."

"Coming where?"

"A bargain will be needed. And *I* won't be the one paying for it."

I stood, finally releasing his hand. "Deal. Let's go."

Gladiola stood a few paces back, dumbfounded. "I'm not even sure what I just witnessed."

"The question," Sebastian said as he walked past her toward the stairs, "is not how she stands being around me. But how *I* stand being around *her*."

"You'll stay with Aaliyah, right?" I asked as I moved to follow Sebastian. "I don't want to leave her alone."

"But I—" Gladiola stammered.

"Please don't make me whimper like a dog again, kay thanks, bye!" I practically jogged after Sebastian before Gladiola could argue, though I heard her murmuring curses under her breath as I rushed down the stairs.

I caught up to Sebastian at the door, where he simply gave me a final glare, then walked outside.

Maybe I was getting the hang of working with a devil after all.

7

"So THIS PERSON we are going to meet, is she a friend of yours?" I watched Sebastian out the corner of my eye as we walked down the street. Our destination was only a few blocks away, or so he claimed. Even so, with all the walking we had done tonight, my feet were going to be aching in the morning.

"An acquaintance, nothing more." His words were clipped.

"An acquaintance I'm going to have to bargain with?" I pressed, apprehension thick in my throat.

Devils weren't the only creatures who would bargain with humans. Fae and goblins both had just as many tricks up their sleeves. I wasn't sure which of the three I was hoping for. Couldn't anyone just take cash these days?

"She does not give her potions for free. And she has no use for more money."

I frowned at his words echoing my own thoughts. "And what exactly does she have use for?"

We turned onto a street of low buildings, most lit up with old school neon. A few cloth banners fluttered in the air, offering various goods and services. I suspected that during the day there would be stalls outside for the general public, but at night... The darkened buildings had an ominous feel, and there was a hint of residual magic in the air.

He stopped outside of one particularly ominous building with a purple potion bottle glowing in neon through the front window. "In all likelihood she will want a sample of your magic."

I stared at him. "A sample?"

His eyes slid toward mine. "I told you, you would have to pay."

"Yeah, but I didn't know what I would be paying with. This feels like a trick." I crossed my arms, suddenly feeling a chill even through my jacket.

"You begged me like a small dog to bring you here."

I wrinkled my nose. "Good point."

He gestured toward the glass and metal door. A heavy purple curtain hung across the inside, and the blinds were drawn behind the neon sign, blocking any view of the interior.

I studied Sebastian's face for a moment longer, but he was right. I had asked him to bring me here, and Aaliyah's life was hanging in the balance. I couldn't back out now. I grabbed the door and tugged it open, jingling the bell attached to the inside.

I was met with a smell so acrid it nearly made me choke. I waved my hand in front of my face, trying to shoo away the smoke. Ringo scurried down the sleeve of my coat and back into my messenger bag, coughing and sputtering.

When my vision finally cleared, I took in a long gleaming countertop with shelves of filled bottles behind it. There was a door open to a back room—the source of the smoke. An antique lamp on the countertop flickered as if irritated.

"Who's there?" A female voice called from the back room.

Since Sebastian was standing next to me like a useless statue, I stepped toward the counter. "Hello?"

A woman peeked out of the room. Her red hair was cropped into a messy pixie cut, leaving her soft, rounded features bare. She looked like she was in her forties, but it was always hard to tell with different creatures. Judging by her simple white T-shirt and baggy jeans, my guess was she wasn't one of the really old ones. They tended to cling to more refined styles of dress.

"Well? What do you want?" Her eyes darted from me to Sebastian. "Oh hey, I know you. It's been a while." She stepped fully out of the back room and walked toward the counter, suddenly interested. "Tell me you're here for another potion. The sample you gave me last time did all sorts of crazy things."

Great, he had brought me to a mad woman. And he was simply looking at me, waiting for me to do the talking.

"Actually, I'm the one who needs something." When she continued observing Sebastian, I had to wave my hand to get her attention.

She looked me up and down. "Oh. You don't look very interesting."

"Gee, thanks." I approached the counter. "I know someone who I think has been poisoned. Sebastian believes you might be able to offer a cure."

She looked at him again, one eyebrow raised. "A cure for an unknown poison? My, you do think highly of me, don't you?"

When Sebastian still didn't answer her, I cleared my throat. "Can you do it?"

She sighed, leaning her elbows on the countertop. "I have a sort of all purpose concoction. It will work for most of the common poisons, but not everything. And if the person poisoned isn't human, it might work differently."

I glanced at Sebastian, wondering just how much I should tell this woman, but he was being absolutely no help. "She's a nymph," I explained. "We don't know exactly what happened to her, but she has no visible injuries. She couldn't walk, and was incredibly weak.

Eventually she lost consciousness, and her heart rate is starting to slow."

She pursed her lips and tilted her head at my words. "I might be able to work with that." She gave me a pointed look. "But it doesn't come cheap." Her eyes drifted once more to Sebastian.

"What do you want?" I asked.

"Your soul, of course." Before I could respond, she laughed. "Oh, wait, I guess that's *his* thing." She rolled her eyes again toward Sebastian, who was finally starting to show his irritation.

Not seeming to notice, she continued. "What I want depends on what kind of magic you have. You do have magic, don't you? I highly doubt this guy would be toting around a *lowly human.*"

Sebastian sighed heavily. "Isadora is human. She can't tell what type of magic you have. She can only use alchemy to include it in her concoctions."

Isadora lifted a hand to cover one side of her mouth as she whispered, "He says human like it's such a dirty word, doesn't he?"

Sebastian huffed again. "I'm going to wait outside." Rather than using the door, he disappeared in a cloud of darkness.

Isadora watched the darkness slowly dissipating from the center of her shop. "Why are the handsome ones always such assholes?"

"You have no idea," I laughed.

Her curious eyes lifted back to my face. "So what

are you doing with him? You don't seem—" she wiggled her fingers in the air, "*evil*."

"A contract of convenience," I said vaguely. "And no offense, can we get back to the potion? The nymph seemed stable, but I'm not sure how long she has."

"Of course," she chirped. "Let the bargaining begin. First, I'll need to know what *flavor* you are. As Mr. tall, dark, and arrogant already explained, I'm human. I can't read your magic, I can only use it in my experiments."

"I am a night runner," I said. "Half celestial."

"Ooh, star magic." Her eyes widened as she glanced down at my messenger bag. "And what precisely is that?"

Ringo gasped, then retreated back into the bag.

"You've never seen a goblin?"

Her brows lifted. "Human, remember? I've had a few dealings with people with some goblin blood, but it's not like I can go to the Bogs." She put her elbows on the counter again, peering at the bag as if she could see Ringo through the fabric. "I'll give you all the potions you want if you let me keep that little guy."

"He's not for sale." Was this woman nuts?

She straightened. "Worth a try. Some of your fancy star magic will do." She jerked her head toward the back room. "Let's go."

Giving my bag a reassuring pat to let Ringo know he wasn't going anywhere, I followed her back into her work room. A few lamps lit rows upon rows of bottles, some filled and some empty. There was a small refrigerator next to a clinical looking workstation with a sink in the center. I spotted a few metal tools that looked suspiciously like torture devices, and wondered if this was how Sebastian planned to finally be rid of me. Maybe he was tired of all my failed realm jumping attempts.

Isadora grabbed an empty bottle from one of the shelves, the bulbous base the size of a softball, then she reached for a separate jar filled with a milky liquid. She turned toward me, extending the jar in front of my face. "This is the carrier, and no, I'm not gonna tell you what's in it. It's a proprietary secret. All you need to know is that it has the ability to infuse itself with magic, thus making it a liquid and not just energy. Once the magic is a liquid, I can study its properties and use it in different potions, which I then sell to the highest bidder."

I peered skeptically at the milky substance. "And how do we meld the magic and the liquid to begin with?"

She scoffed. "How should I know? You're the magic user here. Wiggle your nose, do a little dance, or whatever else it is you do to call your fancy powers forth."

Should I tell her that lately my magic mostly reacted to making out with hot men?

Probably not.

"Okay... so I put the magic in the bottle, then you give me the poison cure?"

"Exactly." She winked. "And don't worry about me

stiffing you. I'm not about to run off with your payment when you have a devil waiting outside."

"Okay, sure." This was the weirdest thing ever. I took the milky substance from her, then unscrewed the lid of the jar. I gave it a sniff then instantly jerked my head back, my eyes watering.

Isadora smirked, then turned toward her workstation. She started stirring something purple and viscous in a metal bowl. "Take your time, star lady."

I looked down into the jar, trying to figure out how best to put my magic into it. But it wasn't like I could create things out of nothing, not like Sebastian's shadows. My magic was just inside me.

"So how do you know Sebastian?" I asked as I quietly racked my brain.

"He came to me for a potion a year or so back." She continued her aggressive stirring as she spoke. "And I never forget a face. Especially not a face like *that*."

I smelled the liquid in the jar again, more cautiously this time. "What kind of potion?"

"It was for a sick human, if I recall correctly."

I lifted my brows at her, though with her back to me, she didn't see it. Sebastian wouldn't care about a sick human. But maybe he had done it to secure a contract. Still, I stored the information amongst the other intel I had slowly been gathering on him. It wasn't much, but I would take whatever I could get, because I knew eventually I would need the upper hand. That was how it worked with devils. *Always*.

I placed my palm over the open jar, trying to summon a bit of my magic. When nothing happened, I added the visual of Gabriel with his shirt off into my mind. It was a nice picture, but it still didn't spark little stars around my fingertips.

Isadora paused her stirring to glance back at me. "You alright there?"

"Fine," I muttered, closing my eyes and pressing my palm more firmly over the jar of liquid. Gods, I did not want to owe Sebastian *another* favor. They were really starting to pile up.

I scrunched up my face, straining. Here I was, able to transport myself to different places, but I couldn't summon a lick of magic into a jar.

With a heavy sigh, I removed my hand from the opening, then reached into my back pocket, withdrawing Sebastian's card.

Isadora had turned to watch me, arms crossed and head tilted to one side.

I rubbed my finger across the card, focusing my attention on it. At least this bit of magic was simple enough. The card pulsed with heat, then Isadora gasped as Sebastian appeared just behind me.

"You rang?"

I sighed, turning toward him. I lifted the empty jar, my eyes pleading.

"You're not going to start whining like a dog again, are you?"

"Maybe?"

He stepped toward me, and I reflexively stepped back. "What are you doing?"

"You asked for help, dear Eva. I'm giving it."

He wrapped his hand around the jar, trapping my fingers, then slid his other hand around my waist, pulling me against him. Then he kissed me.

8

I STIFFENED MOMENTARILY, then my body melted as Sebastian's tongue delved into my mouth. He still had one hand gripping mine around the jar, while his other hand kneaded my lower back. I made a small sound in the back of my throat and he gripped me tighter, pressing my hips against him hard enough to lift my heels off the floor.

Magic course through me like electrical currents in my chest, answering his call. It was different with him than with Mistral or Gabriel, my magic like a dark yawning cavern inside me, opening up to swallow us both whole.

My lashes fluttered against my cheeks as he drank me down, reacting to sudden pulsing lights at the edge of my awareness. Sebastian's hand slipped underneath the edge of my shirt, stroking up my bare back.

The touch made heat pool between my thighs, but

at the same time reactivated my only remaining brain cell, reminding me where we were and just who I was kissing. I pulled back, breaking the kiss, but his grip on my bare back kept me against him.

I tried to us my hand that wasn't wrapped around the jar to shield my eyes from the red and purple aurora emanating from my body, then realized it was coming from my fingers too. I had never seen a true aurora in person, only in pictures, but I knew that's what I was seeing now. And it was coming from *me*.

Sebastian lifted our hands still joined around the jar to show me that the liquid had turned from milky white to a deep, glowing magenta.

Isadora let out a low whistle. "Magic *and* a show. My, aren't I a lucky girl?"

I looked up at Sebastian, still holding me against him. There was heat in his eyes, but something else. Something I was uncomfortable seeing in anyone's eyes but a lover.

Isadora cautiously approached, taking the jar from our hands before screwing a metal lid onto it. She took it back to her shelves, plucking a different bottle from a row of others identical to it.

Sebastian finally released me, and when I looked up at him, whatever I had seen before in his expression was gone. The light around me dimmed, then slowly faded.

Isadora returned to us, handing me a bottle filled with glittering lavender liquid. "This should fix your nymph. And please, come see me *any* time."

"That's it?" I asked, feeling a little shaken.

She shrugged. "I get plenty of cash from the humans I sell to. What you have is far more valuable than cash."

Sebastian placed a hand at the small of my back, just the light touch making me want to throw myself into his arms again. "It's late. We should go."

Isadora's eyes sparkled with curiosity, but she didn't ask any further questions. Instead she adopted a fake drawl and said, "Y'all come back now, ya hear?" With a little wave, she turned back to her workstation, admiring the jar of my magic.

Sebastian guided me back outside.

The noise of the streets had quieted considerably at the late hour. "Should I be concerned about her having some of my magic?"

"What she does with it is not our problem." He started walking without a single glance back at Isadora's shop.

He didn't seem to want to talk, and maybe it was for the best. Because what the hell was that kiss? It wasn't the first one, of course, but things had definitely escalated, and I didn't understand it. Just as I didn't understand how Mistral could call stars from my fingertips, while Gabriel called forth a warm glow. And now Sebastian could bring about a friggin aurora. It was like my magic was choosing them for different reasons, but I didn't have any say in it.

The goblins I didn't mind. But Sebastian?

I watched his broad shoulders as he led the way down the street, itching to know more. Itching to know if *he* knew more. He knew he could call my magic, but did he realize exactly what would happen back there?

My bag shifted against me as Ringo tossed aside the flap to look up at me. He had his arms wrapped around the antidote I had slid in there after Isadora gave it to me. "The bottle feels warm," he whispered. "Warmer than it should. Are you sure it's safe to give to her?"

I frowned. I had been so intent on gaining the antidote, I hadn't stopped to question if it might do more harm than good. "We don't really have any other options, unless we call her sister. Which would be bad. She would come here, and if anyone knew they interacted, Aaliyah would be cast out, just like Seraphina."

"But what about whoever poisoned her?" he whispered, his words barely audible as a car whizzed by on the dark, damp street.

"Hopefully we can find out more about it when she wakes." I picked up my pace to catch up with Sebastian, anxious to get back.

I wasn't sure what I had expected with taking a devil on my delivery, but this certainly had not been the night I had bargained for.

))✦✿✦✿✦((

GLADIOLA RUSHED OVER AS we reached the top of the stairs. "It's about time! Her breathing has become labored. Did you get the antidote?" Her wide eyes darted back and forth between us.

I glared at Sebastian. "I thought you said we had time!"

He shrugged, his eyes on the sofa at the other end of the room. "She is not dead, so we had time."

Shaking my head, I hurried over to Aaliyah, kneeling beside the sofa. Ringo handed me the antidote from within my bag and I unscrewed the lid.

Gladiola peered dubiously at the glittering liquid. "That looks more like a party trick than an antidote. Are you sure you got the right thing?"

"Just help me tilt her head back," I huffed.

She did as I asked, gently moving Aaliyah's hair out of the way so she could tilt her head, making her mouth fall open.

I dribbled some of the liquid into the nymph's mouth, but it started to pool at the back of her throat. "Ringo—"

But he was already hopping onto Aaliyah's chest. He worked his little blue paws at her throat, and she convulsed, swallowing the liquid.

Gladiola had moved to the head of the couch to more easily maintain Aaliyah's position. "Wow, I've only seen people do that with animals."

"Hey, whatever works," I muttered.

I poured more liquid in, and Ringo got her to swallow again. It was a painstakingly long process, but eventually we got her to drink the entire small bottle, which I hoped was right. I had forgotten to ask Isadora about dosage.

I set the empty bottle aside, and we all waited, watching her. Well, all of us except Sebastian. He had disappeared somewhere else in the apartment.

"Well," Gladiola said after a while. "At least she's breathing more easily now. I guess we won't really know if it worked until she wakes up. *If* she wakes up."

"Yeah." I crossed my legs to sit more comfortably, glancing around for Sebastian. "I guess we're in for a long night."

"Mistral will want to know what happened."

Guilt clawed at the back of my throat. I was such a jerk for avoiding him just because I was embarrassed. "You should go tell him what happened. Tell him I won't be able to make it tonight, but I'll come tomorrow, after I'm finished at Emerald Heights." I caught sight of Sebastian out the corner of my eye as I said it. He was leaning against the wall with his arms crossed, and I wasn't sure how long he had been there.

Gladiola gave him a wary glance. "You're going to stay here with *him?*" she whispered.

The thought made me uncomfortable, but if something went wrong with Aaliyah, he would probably just let her die. And he was right earlier, someone had tried to kill the nymph. I couldn't bring that kind of trouble on Braxton again.

"I'll be fine," I said finally.

She gave me a knowing look. "That's not exactly what I'm worried about."

Yeah, her and me both.

I STIRRED another spoonful of rice into my to go container of butter chicken. That was the beauty of living in the city, you could get takeout at any time of the night. I sat cross-legged in front of the sofa, keeping an eye on Aaliyah.

Ringo huddled beside me on the floor, snout deep in a styrofoam container of curried potatoes. There was a lamp on beside the sofa, but the rest of the apartment was dark, save the distant lights from the city far below.

"You're going to be useless tomorrow in Emerald Heights if you stay up all night."

I glanced back at Sebastian. "I'm not going to sleep.'"

It had been an ongoing argument over the past hour. I wanted to make sure Aaliyah would be okay, and I didn't trust Sebastian to watch her.

"She is resting peacefully now. Clearly Isadora's concoction worked."

Had he had doubts? I was once again tempted to ask about how he met Isadora, but the irritation pinching his features let me know he wouldn't be telling the truth regardless. And he would *never* swear a bargain of truth like Mistral. He had far too much to hide.

I took another bite of my food, fighting a yawn. Tomorrow would indeed be rough.

With zero warning, Sebastian was suddenly beside me, yanking me up by one arm while grabbing my messenger bag with his free hand.

"Hey!" I kept a death grip on my food as he dragged me into an adjoining bedroom.

Soft lighting blossomed of its own accord, and I couldn't quite tell where it was coming from. The room was simple, but *expensive*. And were those silk sheets?

Ringo scurried in after us, stopping near my ankles.

Sebastian finally released my arm. "If there are any issues with the nymph, I will wake you."

Clutching my food, I turned toward him. "Do you swear it?"

He rolled his eyes. "I'll even add it to the contract."

"In exchange for what?"

"In exchange for you not being absolutely useless tomorrow. We don't have all the time in the world, Eva. We're not the only ones trying to find your mother. Someone else will manage it."

I squirmed where I stood. He was right. I was taking too long to learn. If someone else found my mom first—

"Do we have a deal?"

I pouted. "Fine. I'll sleep." Gripping my food in one hand, I lifted a finger toward his face. "But you better wake me if there are any issues."

He looped my messenger bag over my extended

arm, stepped back, then shut the door, leaving me and Ringo alone in his bedroom.

I took another bite of my food as I approached the bed. Ringo hopped up, fluffing his fur before diving onto one of the silk pillows. The pillow nearly swallowed him up, leaving just his tufted ears visible.

I smirked. "Make yourself comfortable."

"Devils don't eat goblins." His head appeared as he let out a big yawn, then he buried his face in the silk.

Shaking my head, I set my food down on a side table that probably cost more than my rent, then walked into the adjoining bathroom. The bathtub was definitely not one you would find in a standard apartment. I could practically swim in it. More soft light bloomed around me, showing me my face in the gilded mirror. Luckily I had started carrying toiletries in my messenger bag since I was too often ending up not at home.

I brushed my teeth and washed my face, thinking about tomorrow, and thinking about going to the Bogs.

And also thinking about that gods damned kiss back at Isadora's shop.

9

I RAN AS if my life depended on it, and maybe it did. But I didn't know what I was running from, just some dark, amorphous shape. My breath hissed through my lungs, my heart pounding. Pounding so loud it was all I could hear. *Bang. Bang. Bang.* I was choking on my own heartbeat—

I sat bolt upright in a strange bed with silk sheets. As soon as I sat up, a soft glow emanated from the ceiling, showing me the room at Sebastian's apartment, and Ringo fast asleep on the pillow beside mine.

The banging continued, and I found myself wondering how I had ever thought it was my heartbeat, even in a dream. The realization didn't stop me from needing to catch my breath for a moment, each distant *bang* jolting me.

Pushing my sweaty hair out of my face, I threw back the sheets, slid on my boots, then clomped toward the door. I opened it, expecting Sebastian outside doing something irritating, but he was simply sitting on a chair adjacent the sofa, the dark city skyline visible behind him. He had one ankle draped across one knee, and an old leather bound book in hand.

"Don't you hear that?" I waved my hands to get his attention.

His eyes remained on his book. "Of course I hear it."

"Aren't you going to do anything about it?"

"No."

Shaking my head, I walked past the kitchen toward the sound of the banging, realizing it was someone at the door below. I looked down the stairs, narrowing my eyes. The door outside was hidden, so only someone who knew what to look for would be able to knock, at least that's what I assumed.

I glanced back at Sebastian.

Bobbing his foot, he turned another page in his book.

"Devils," I muttered, then marched down the stairs. Whatever charm or illusion had created them must have been made to close the space for sound too, or else the banging shouldn't have been as loud.

I reached the door. At first it was a solid door, then I blinked, and there was a peephole for me to peer through. I wrinkled my nose, not entirely trusting it. Of course Sebastian would have a place like this. Though I had a feeling this was just a hideaway, not his main home, because there was hardly anything here.

I leaned against the door, looking out just as the knocking resumed. I watched a strong bare arm, its brown skin coated with misty rain, pounding on the wood outside. Attached to the arm was a rather unhappy looking goblin. Gladiola must have told him where to knock.

I opened the door before he could finish his apparent task of pounding it into wood pulp. "Humans *do* sleep. You know that, right?"

His black hair hung in damp strands around his chiseled features. Even with irritation creasing his brow, he looked downright scrumptious all damp and sulky. A dark green T-shirt strained across his muscled chest, paired with black jeans. "Gladiola told me what happened with the nymph. I didn't think you would be sleeping."

I looked out into the alleyway, glancing in both directions. We were alone, but still it probably wasn't the best place to discuss things. I stepped back, gesturing for him to come inside.

He did, dripping water onto the wood floor as he loomed over me. He shut the door behind him before sliding a palm over the wood, observing it closely.

I wondered if it felt like he had been knocking on brick or a softer wooden door that whole time.

"Why are you here, Gabriel? I told Gladiola to let you know I couldn't come tonight."

His dark eyes were like flex of onyx, his mouth a grim line. "Someone wants this nymph, and you're harboring her."

I crossed my arms, not sure whether to be irritated or touched that he was feeling so protective. "I'm in an entirely hidden apartment with a devil. I think I'm fine."

He lowered his chin, giving me his patented *you're being very silly* look.

"I'm really fine," I pressed.

"After what happened with the fae—"

"You're the one who got stabbed, not me."

His chin tipped even lower. "An elf tried to slit your throat."

I rolled my eyes, then turned to head up the stairs. I knew he wasn't going anywhere, so we may as well be comfortable. He followed me up, then we both stood there looking at Sebastian in his chair, not acknowledging either of us.

I cleared my throat.

Sebastian lowered his book, giving me a pointed look. "You're *supposed* to be sleeping."

I raised my hands. "Yes, I'm going to be useless in Emerald Heights tomorrow, I get it."

His eyes drifted back down to the book in his hands. "Your nymph has begun to stir. Perhaps you can divine where she would like to be delivered so we can get this over with."

I looked at Gabriel, then hurried toward the couch.

Ringo finally came scurrying out of the room, crawling up onto my shoulder as soon as I knelt down.

Aaliyah had her back to me, and seemed to be sleeping peacefully. But Sebastian was right, she had repositioned herself on her own. I lightly shook her shoulder.

She groaned, then turned over, rubbing eyes that quickly grew three sizes larger as she stared at me, then the big goblin behind me. "W-what happened?" She started to sit up, then winced, holding a hand to her head.

"Take it easy," I soothed. "We think you were poisoned. We brought you here to recover."

She lowered her hand, though she still looked pained. "Poison? No, it's a curse. They caught my uncle outside of our territory and that's what happened to him —punishment for leaving our realm." She pinched her brow, taking a few deep breaths, and when she looked up at me, her eyes were clearer. "I didn't think anyone had followed me, but once I reached the park, something hit me. I couldn't tell what happened, but I was suddenly horribly weak, and I could barely think straight."

"Well a poison antidote is what saved you."

Aaliyah stared at me, clearly not comprehending what I was saying.

I sat crosslegged on the floor, scooting a little closer to the couch, trying to look harmless. "Maybe you could start from the beginning and tell me exactly what happened."

Aaliyah looked past me at Gabriel again.

"No one here is going to hurt you," I said calmly. "Just start from the beginning. We'll help you figure this out."

Sebastian snorted, earning him a sharp look from me, which he didn't seem to care about in the slightest.

Aaliyah gave him a wary look, but finally, cleared her throat and began her tale.

)}♦●◉●●●{(

GABRIEL, Sebastian, and I walked back down the stairs, leaving Ringo with Aaliyah. Magic popped in my ears as Sebastian made a barrier around us, preventing any eavesdropping.

Gabriel's expression was grim as he glanced back up the stairs. "Her story sounds like a child's tale."

"Yeah, well so does my life lately," I sighed. "It doesn't mean it isn't true. At the very least, she believes it. *Something* happened to her."

"She was likely poisoned earlier." Sebastian stroked his chin in thought. At some point during her story, he had finally become interested in the mystery of it all. I knew he didn't care what happened to her, but he enjoyed a good puzzle. "It hit her in the park, so she believes she was attacked by a curse at that time, but it could have simply been a slow-moving poison. If she came from her family's dwelling, it may have even happened there."

"That still doesn't tell us who did it," I said.

He lowered his hand from his chin, waving me off. "Nor is it really our concern. Return her to her people so we can get on with our day."

"If you simply drop her off," Gabriel grumbled, "someone else might try to kill her."

Fire flashed in Sebastian's eyes. "She now knows she was poisoned. She can tell her family what happened and they can protect her. Nymphs look after their own. It is an absolute necessity when they choose to live in the city."

"You have no concern for what's best for her. Nor what's best for Eva."

Sebastian lifted a brow. "And *you* know what's best for Eva?"

I threw up my arms before they could go any further. "We can't keep doing this! We all need to be able to work together, and not just in regards to Aaliyah. We have the *same* goal. It only makes sense to tolerate each other."

Sebastian tilted his head, his dark eyes still on Gabriel. "I tolerate *Crispin* admirably."

"Yeah," I huffed, "but the contract with King Francis also involves a goblin. Once we have the Realm Breaker, one goblin can go on an exploratory mission to their homeland. To see if whatever this darkness King Francis was talking about has spread."

Sebastian crossed his arms, leaning back against the wall. If he was worried about the big irritated goblin potentially grabbing him and throwing him out the door, he didn't show it. "Just because a goblin will be allowed use of the blade does not mean they must help prior to that point."

Annoyed, I put a hand on Gabriel's chest, focusing on my emotions for him. It wasn't hard with everybody all worked up, and him looking sexy as hell with those brooding, angry eyes. He relaxed against my touch, and my palm began to glow against him.

Sebastian watched us blandly.

"With Mistral," I said, "it's stars. I don't know what's going on with me but it's like you said." I stared Sebastian down with my hand still on Gabriel's chest. "What happened with Mistral made my magic grow. I don't know why it has chosen each of you, but it has, and it scares the hell out of me." I took a deep, steadying breath. "But I want to find my mom before someone kills her. So we are all going to work together to figure this out."

Sebastian studied us, calculating.

Long moments ticked by, Gabriel's heart beating steadily beneath my palm.

Finally, Sebastian gave a slight nod. "Very well. I will speak with King Francis." With that, he disappeared in a cloud of darkness, taking his eavesdropping bubble with him.

I opened and closed my mouth, trying to get my ears

to pop at the sudden pressure change, then removed my hand from Gabriel to rub the side of my jaw. "Well, that went over more easily than expected."

"He wants you to be more powerful, Eva." Gabriel's voice was a low rumble. "He will do whatever it takes, whether it's something you prefer, or not." He turned and started up the stairs, clearly irritated.

"And why are *you* mad now?" I asked after him. "I'm trying to get you a free pass into Emerald Heights."

Just a few steps up, he paused and looked back at me. "Have you thought, perhaps, that it is not your magic that has chosen each of us," he gripped the railing to lean closer, "but you?"

He met my eyes for a long moment, then turned and continued up the stairs.

"What the hell is that supposed to mean?" I muttered.

But there was no one around to answer.

10

"Are you sure you'll be okay here?" I asked, squinting against the early morning light.

Aaliyah huddled in my hooded sweatshirt, her shoulders hunched as she looked at the gates to the small park. We were several blocks from the lake, and I couldn't even imagine her walking there herself at night. But she had, with poison in her system no less. And now Gabriel and I were dropping her off, since Sebastian hadn't returned from his talk with King Francis.

"I'll be safe once I'm inside." Her eyes darted toward me, avoiding Gabriel standing at my side.

"But you were probably poisoned by someone in there," I whispered.

Nymph families were usually large, even when they broke off to live within cities. They would take over parks, but you would never actually see their dwellings.

Like night runners, they could shift just enough into another pocket realm where they actually lived.

She met my eyes, then gave a slight nod. "I will tell my parents. They'll know what to do. Just please don't tell anyone what I was doing in the park. They can't know about the packages from Seraphina."

My jaw fell open at her words. "Oh, wow, I actually forgot about the package." I started to pull the small parcel out of my messenger bag.

She lifted a delicate, long-fingered hand. She looked so frail and vulnerable in her long white dress, my sweatshirt way too big for her. "Keep it. I can't bring it back with me."

"But—"

"It's okay. My sister will understand."

I doubted Seraphina would understand about *anything* that had transpired, but I didn't argue.

Aaliyah had already turned her attention back to the park.

"Be safe," I said.

"I will." She smiled. "No one will ever believe that I met not only a celestial, but a devil and a goblin." Her eyes lowered as Ringo popped his head out of my bag. "*Two* goblins. Well meaning strangers who happened upon me entirely by chance."

"Yep, we were just taking a nice moonlight stroll. Found an unconscious nymph and took her home."

"Thank you," she said again, then turned and walked toward the park.

Gabriel and I watched her until she was safe beyond the gates. Or as safe as she could be with a poisoner waiting somewhere inside.

Gabriel stood close enough for his chest to press against the back of my shoulder. "I have a bad feeling just letting her go like this."

I shrugged. "So do I, but short of holding her hostage, there's not a lot we can do. I'm going to call her sister though, see if she knows anything about what happened."

But first, coffee. Then home to shower.

I glanced at Gabriel as we started walking. "What's your opinion on the city bus?"

He placed his hand at the small of my back, pulling me closer as a bike messenger whizzed by. "Tedious, but useful."

"Good, then let's go." I hesitated. "Unless you need to check back in with Mistral?"

"A messenger will be sent to your apartment if there are any issues."

I shook my head, smiling as we reached the bus stop. "You know, phones are pretty useful." I held up my watch, not exactly a phone, but close enough.

"They do not work in the Citadel. Too far from any phone towers."

The shaded bench was full, so we both stood near everyone else waiting. "Yeah but you could *have* a phone, and so could Mistral. Then a messenger could venture far enough to get service to text you."

He humored me with a small smile. "We have never had much use for being out in the city, until now."

"Until me, you mean?"

He continued smiling as the bus pulled up and opened its doors.

"So have I convinced you to get a phone?"

He waited for me to walk up the steps ahead of him. "I'll see what I can do."

Everyone already on the bus probably thought I was crazy for the way I was grinning. But it would be nice to be able to text. There would be no need for random late night apartment visits.

Of course, I didn't particularly mind those, at least from Gabriel.

We walked toward the back of the bus, and I grabbed one of the loops dangling from the ceiling. Gabriel put an arm around my waist, glaring at anyone who came too near.

I heard paper tearing in my messenger bag and shook my head. "We're giving the package back to Seraphina, Ringo."

"But it smells good," he whispered beneath the flap of my bag.

"I'll get you a potato pastry on the way home if you stay out of it."

All paper tearing ceased. I've got a few odd looks for talking to my bag, all short-lived with Gabriel glaring behind me. I checked my watch as the bus started moving. We should have time for a stop at my favorite cafe before we had to meet Sebastian in Emerald Heights. Maybe I'd even get an extra coffee to put in a thermos for the road. Because being in a room with Sebastian, Gabriel, and Crispin at the same time was *definitely* going to require extra caffeine.

⁙

GABRIEL LEANED near my shoulder as I pointed to different pastries behind the display case. "Why are you choosing so many?"

"—and two of those," I finished, pointing to the spiced pumpkin croissants. Autumn was finally on its way, and I was all for it. I paid, then shuffled aside to wait for our coffees and pastries.

"First of all," I said to Gabriel as I pointed toward a freshly open table, "when one has a werewolf roommate, one must always order extra pastries." I sat down, brushing aside a few crumbs as Gabriel took the chair right next to mine instead of across from me. "Second, I feel like our time in Emerald Heights is going to be incredibly awkward, and I would like sugar to stuff into my mouth at any opportune moments."

Gabriel watched a couple half-elves hurrying past us toward another open table, their coffees already in hand. He turned his serious eyes back to me. "If Sebastian is actually going to convince the elf king to allow me into his realm, he has motivations of his own. He does nothing to simply accommodate."

"Obviously, but you do have a right to be there." I had a thought. "And you might even be able to help me out with something."

His brow furrowed.

"Oh don't look so worried." I waved him off. Glancing around, I leaned forward and lowered my voice. "My old boss is trying to get some information on my mom, but she has a crush on one of the elves. If you get a free pass into Emerald Heights, you might be able to ask around a bit. My *lessons* take hours. There should be time."

"Cannot Elena do so?"

I started to shrug, then saw the barista holding up our coffee carrier and bag of pastries. Gabriel beat me to it, taking both in hand. Together we walked toward the door, which he opened with one elbow, holding it for me until I was outside. I took the pastry bag from him because I was a big girl. I could carry my own pastries.

I finished my shrug as we started walking. "To answer your question about Elena, I'm going to ask her too. But she's young, and my boss thinks this elf is old school nobility. I don't think Elena spends much time chatting up his type."

He lifted a brow as we stopped at the crosswalk. "And I do?"

I cringed. "Good point. Sometimes I forget you haven't been around as long as Mistral." The light changed, and I glanced at him as we started walking.

"How did you come to be his..." I waved one hand in the air, searching for the right word.

"Vassal," he finished for me. "I have been as such since I was a teenager. Our mothers were close friends, both having traveled from our home realm, but my mother passed away well before Mistral's."

We hit the sidewalk on the other side, and turned in the direction of my apartment. "Can I ask what happened?"

For a moment, I thought he might not answer, then he said, "The realm was unstable, even when Queen Maeve was alive. Wild goblin magic was never meant to be caged. My mother was caught in an incident not unlike the one you saved us from, only water was involved. She drowned."

I gripped his arm, stopping him from walking so he looked at me. "I'm sorry. I know what it's like to lose a parent."

Pulling me away from the foot traffic, he lifted my hand and kissed my knuckles, sending a delightful shiver right between my legs. "It was a long time ago, there is nothing to be sorry about."

He stared into my eyes long enough to make me blush, then kept my hand in his as we continued walking. "I have been by Mistral's side ever since," he finished.

"And now you've been by mine. Leaving him vulnerable."

His fingers flexed around mine. "He asked me to

come. The older goblins are different. They have seen much in their long lives, and they do not tend to get attached as easily as some of us." He glanced at me. "But it's not just about your magic and what you represent to him. He has grown quite... *fond* of you."

There was that damn blush again. "Well I'm quite fond of him." I darted my eyes his way. "And that really doesn't bother you?"

Gabriel kept his eyes on our surroundings as we neared my apartment. "It does not. His life has been one of great burden. I enjoy seeing how he is around you."

We reached the exterior stairs leading up to my humble abode. I looked around for any neighbors, but we were alone, and inside Braxton would probably be there. I leaned close, well aware of Ringo in my satchel, but he had heard plenty already. "I'm nervous to be around both of you at the same time."

"You're embarrassed." There was no accusation in his tone, just a simple statement.

I shrugged, crinkling the pastry bag. "I guess. It's just never a situation I thought I'd end up in."

"Is it a situation you *want* to be in?"

Blushing more furiously than ever, I nodded.

"And what of Sebastian?"

I looked down at my boots. I had no vow of truth with Gabriel, but as usual, I found myself not wanting to lie to him. "He's a pain in the ass, but I can't deny that my magic is drawn to him."

"Or maybe *you're* drawn to him?"

I forced myself to meet his eyes, but I was unsure of what to say. Mostly because I didn't know the truth myself.

He leaned forward, bringing himself down closer to my height. "Your secrets are yours to keep, Eva. The only person you owe your honesty to, is yourself."

I narrowed my eyes at him. "When did you become so wise?"

He chuckled. "I am younger than Mistral, but I'm not *that* young."

He reclaimed my hand and led me up the stairs. I walked silently behind him, not for the first time realizing that I was completely out of my depth.

11

CRISPIN TOOK US IN, his blue eyes seeming to dance as they flitted between us. "An intriguing assortment of test subjects, that's to be sure."

He wore houndstooth pants and a saturated cornflower blue shirt that matched his eyes. He had made an effort to comb his tousled blond hair, but he had already run his fingers through it so many times that it was in complete disarray.

He probably had never expected to see a goblin in his tower, and according to Sebastian, it almost didn't happen. King Francis had been resistant to the idea of a goblin coming in, but when the contract was brought up, he couldn't exactly argue. I had personally made sure the goblins were included.

Only now, I found myself wishing I hadn't pushed for the situation. Now there was one more person to see me fail.

"I'm interested in these magical reactions." Crispin started pacing, still observing us.

I glared at Sebastian, receiving only a shrug in reply. He must have discussed it with Crispin when he came to speak with the king.

The door flew open, and Elena stumbled in. Her bare arms shone with sweat, though her white tank top and tight black jeans appeared pristine. "Sorry I'm late!" She tried to push some loose strands of red hair back into her braid, leaving her pointed ears on full display. "My father had me running all sorts of errands. No doubt trying to keep me away from today's lesson." She grinned at me.

I felt for King Francis. After his daughter had gotten drunk with werewolves and was nearly killed by fae, he had the parental right to worry. Never mind that Elena did exactly as she pleased regardless.

"Actually, I need to talk to you." I stepped away from the guys, grabbing her arm to drag her back out into the hall.

As soon as the door was shut, Elena gave me a mischievous smile. "Is this about the big hunky goblin glaring at everyone? You never told me exactly what happened after you disappeared with him that night."

"Well no—"

"Glaring at everyone except for *you*, of course," she continued as if I hadn't spoken. "Which I don't know why. We fought side by side. Comrades in arms—"

"Elena," I hissed. "We are not here to talk about my sex life."

"Oooh so the sex life exists?"

I pinched my brow and shook my head. "I need a favor. Do you know an elf named Rian?"

Her face screwed up in confusion. "I'm going to need a little bit more to go on than that. There are a lot of elves."

"This one is haughty nobility."

"I spend as little time talking with *that* lot as possible. Why?"

"I have a lead on my mom," I explained, glancing at the closed door, wondering when one of the guys was going to interrupt us. "But I promised I'd get some information on an elf named Rian in return."

Her brows lowered. "You're not planning on killing him, are you?"

I rolled my eyes. "I just need to know if he's seeing anyone, and if not, if he's interested in the female gender. Particularly very tall, powerful females."

Her brows shot up in the other direction.

"Someone has a crush on him," I sighed. "And that someone is trying to find information for me. I was hoping you could take Gabriel and ask around."

One corner of her mouth curled. "I'll gladly ask around, but if you think Crispin will be letting me take Gabriel out of here—" She shook her head. "I was here earlier when Sebastian came with his plan. Now Crispin is very excited about these magical reactions.

And wasn't the whole point of bringing him to explore things further?"

My cheeks flared with heat. Served me right for telling Sebastian anything, but I couldn't exactly be upset. I was the one who had brought up exploring the magical reactions further. The farthest jump I had managed had been in connection to Gabriel, and we had gone all the way across a boundary. I needed that same magic to jump to a near realm. I lowered my eyes, not having any good answer for her, but she figured it out anyways.

"Oh, you're terrified," she laughed.

"Wouldn't you be?"

"Absolutely, but as a simple spectator, I can't wait."

"And this is why I won't talk to you about my sex life," I huffed.

"Eva," she tsked. "I know you were raised around humans and these sort of things are more difficult for you, but you need to remember, it's all just energy. As long as the energy is positive for all involved, there's nothing to be embarrassed about."

I crossed my arms. "I don't see *you* dating anyone."

She wrinkled her nose. "I'm a princess. *Dating* for me means finding my lifelong mate and consort. You should count yourself lucky to have more than one guy drooling after you."

Her words melted my irritation. "So you've *never* dated?"

She crossed her arms, mirroring me, her gaze

darting away. "I've had a few kisses, unbeknownst to my father, but it can be nothing more."

"Warrick will be so disappointed."

Her eyes drifted back to me.

I shook my head. "Never mind. So can you help me find information on Rian?"

"Only if you promise to not send your goblin along with me. Just at least listen to what Crispin has planned."

The fact that I wanted to argue even though it had been my idea to begin with was absolutely ridiculous, but still, I wanted to argue. I knew if I was to discover the secrets to realm jumping, I had to embrace every aspect of my magic, but faced with the guys waiting for me on the other side of the door, I just couldn't quite move my feet.

Grinning mischievously, Elena helped me out by opening the door and shoving me back inside. "It will take me time to find the information you want. So don't rush on my account." She shut the door before I could go after her.

I turned to face the boys, realizing they had been busy. Crispin now had Gabriel and Sebastian both standing near his work table with little medical monitors stuck all over them. Sebastian had removed his jacket and unbuttoned his crisp white shirt, and Gabriel had removed his shirt entirely. They looked like something out of an erotic sci-fi romance.

Gods save us all.

Crispin steepled his fingers like an evil genius, turning toward me. "I have come up with an experiment, dear Eva. And you're probably not going to like it."

))●●●●●((

I STOOD in front of the guys, one hand on Gabriel's chest, and one hand on Sebastian's. Crispin checked his little monitor for any signs of life, then scribbled something in his leather bound journal. He had been monitoring things for a while, and I wasn't sure what he was getting out of all of this.

Even though nothing was happening, Gabriel's steady gaze made me blush. And Sebastian... There was something different in his expression. No teasing. No trying to make me angry for a reaction. He was just *waiting*, his dark eyes hiding far too many secrets.

"Alright," Crispin said, paying more attention to his journal and monitor than any of us. "Try summoning your magic."

I closed my eyes. I was the one who wanted to explore this. I knew my magic wasn't progressing fast enough. I had no desire for power—I had already seen the trouble it could cause—but I needed to find my mother.

I noticed that Gabriel felt a few degrees warmer than Sebastian, which I would have assumed would have been the other way around, considering where

Sebastian was from. And Sebastian's chest was smooth, where Gabriel had a smattering of course hair. "Nothing is happening."

"You're not even trying," Sebastian's voice hummed against my palm. "Everyone came here for *you*, Eva. Do not waste our time."

I would have glared if my eyes were open. "Fine," I huffed.

Not knowing what else to do, I thought of the previous night in Isadora's shop. Of Sebastian's hands gripping me. His tongue expertly stroking mine...

Magic tickled down my arms and into my core, my body suddenly tight with need. My palms warmed, and I felt an invisible tug toward each of the men before me, like there was a thread binding us together. But where had it come from? When had our fates become so intertwined?

I opened my eyes, trying to pull my hands away, but Sebastian gripped my palm against his chest. "You have to stop fighting it, Eva."

My other hand froze inches away from Gabriel's chest. "I'm not fighting anything."

Gabriel gently took my hand and placed it back against his skin. "Yes, you are."

I glared at both of them, not sure what to say.

"Fascinating." Crispin watched his monitor, seemingly oblivious to the tension in the room.

"Keep going," Sebastian urged, still holding my hand.

I searched his face for the usual irritation, but it wasn't there. He was guarded—he was always *guarded* —but the way he held my hand to his chest... For the first time I could almost see how much this all meant to him.

I closed my eyes again, relaxing my hands, letting the magic flow. I thought of Gabriel with me in my bedroom, his hard body pressed against mine, dwarfing me beneath him. His mouth on my skin...his large hands on my breasts...

Pressure built in my chest. I breathed shallowly, daring to open my eyes.

Gabriel watched me with open hunger, almost as if he could tell exactly what I had been thinking about. I lowered my gaze, and my hand was glowing against his chest with soft light. My other hand against Sebastian radiated with a deep reddish purple aurora.

Crispin been moved close to my hand against Gabriel, studying it. "The readings aren't giving me much to go on." His gaze moved from my hand to my face. "May I touch you?" There was nothing suggestive in his tone, just pure curiosity.

Swallowing the lump in my throat, I nodded.

With both my hands occupied, Crispin gently laid his long fingers across my upper chest, just below my collarbone. A cool, white glow emanated. If Gabriel's glow was sunlight, then Crispin's was the moon.

Panicked, I opened my mouth to speak, but nothing came out.

Sebastian observed Crispin's hand, not appearing entirely pleased. "When you saved him from the near realm. He connected with you too."

"Connected?" I choked out.

Crispin and Sebastian looked at each other. "She's a conduit," Crispin said.

Sebastian nodded.

Magic and arousal made my thoughts swim. I could barely think enough to form words. I shook my head, trying to clear my mind. "What does that mean?"

Crispin's fingers stroked my skin and my body reacted. We had never slept together, but it was like my body remembered him. Like he had always been mine.

He studied the glow between us, then lifted his bright blue eyes to mine. "As a night runner, half human, you don't have enough power to fully jump realms. So instead you found yourself four batteries."

I gasped. "Not on purpose!"

The magic was still growing between us. I knew rationally I could just drop my hands, but I couldn't seem to make myself do it. Instead, I wanted more. I wanted to move my hands across their flesh. I wanted to move *lower*.

"Your first true shift," Sebastian's voice was tight, hinting that he was feeling the same mixture of magic and arousal as the rest of us. "The night you saved Braxton. It was after—"

Neither of us had to say it out loud. Sebastian knew

what had happened. He had picked me up from the Bogs the next morning. But he was implying—

"Mistral's magic is the reason I was able to jump to save Braxton." I looked at Gabriel. "And yours the night I brought you to the Bogs."

Sebastian gripped my hand again as I finally managed to make myself lower it. "Crispin and I have been with you every time you've jumped here. I suspected you might be taking from us, and last night confirmed it."

My jaw fell open. "That's why you kissed me at Isadora's shop?"

"I kissed you because that seems to be the key to summoning your magic. But it did also add to my suspicions."

Crispin nodded along with his words. "We thought you needed to practice your skills, but really we were looking at the wrong thing. We just needed to give you more power." He moved his hand along my upper chest, increasing the glow while at the same time making me weak in the knees. If we didn't break contact soon I was going to end up pouncing one of them, consequences be damned.

"So what do we do now?" I rasped.

Crispin observed the glow of his hand against my skin. "We explore things further. You must try using our magic to bring us somewhere else."

Fear lanced through me, dampening my arousal. "But what if I get us stuck somewhere?"

Crispin smiled softly, that damned charming smile. I had come to care for him in the short time we'd known each other, and I really didn't want him to get stuck in some dark in between place. "We'll all be together," he soothed. "You'll be able to get us back out."

I looked at Sebastian, who smiled wickedly, then at Gabriel, who simply nodded. They were all willing to try this. Hells, it was the sole reason we were here.

But I was afraid. This magic was so new to me, and I didn't fully trust it.

Gabriel gripped my hand against his chest again, giving it a reassuring squeeze.

Meeting his baleful gaze one last time, I closed my eyes. I let the magic flow through us, and I pictured a copse of trees I had seen through one of the palace windows. Somewhere not too far, not too dangerous, and mostly safe from prying eyes. The magic built as soon as I released control. I could feel it flowing between me and the guys. The shift was coming, making me feel lightheaded—

A loud banging behind me made me jump. I looked back at Elena as she came into the room ranting about nobles, my hands lowering from Gabriel and Sebastian in surprise. But it was too late, the shift had already begun.

The next thing I knew, I was falling. Then my body hit *hard* against damp soil and green grass. I tried to exhale but it came out as a stifled groan instead. Sunlight warmed my cheeks and made me squint my eyes as I sat up with another groan, looking around.

Crispin was sprawled in the grass beside me, but just him. Gabriel and Sebastian were nowhere to be seen.

"Shit," I panted. "Where are we?"

Crispin sat up with a pained expression, rubbing his head. He looked around. "Well the good news is, we are still in Emerald Heights."

I furrowed my brow. "And the bad news?"

"I have no idea *where* in Emerald Heights we are."

12

Gabriel

THE DEVIL BUTTONED up his shirt with sharp, irritated movements. "Wait here. I'll find her."

I clenched my hands into fists, wanting nothing more than to throw him out the window. "She told me you're calling card doesn't work beyond boundaries." If this blasted devil disappeared on me, leaving me no way to find Eva—

And he did just that, leaving nothing but a cloud of darkness behind.

Elena took a step back as I turned my glare toward her. She lifted her hands. "I'm sorry! I was just coming to complain about the nobility. I didn't think you would all be jumping realms already!"

"We don't know that they jumped realms." I

snatched my T-shirt from the table then tugged it back on.

This had been such a bad idea. I thought if I came here with her, I could watch over her. But I seemed to only get her into more trouble and not less.

I pointed a finger at the elf. "We are going to search for her. You'll stay with me and make sure no one tries to bar my way."

Her green eyes were so large I thought they might pop out of her head. "Of course! This is nothing new, I assure you. She usually doesn't get far. We'll find her in no time."

"She was drawing magic from three of us this time." I strode past her toward the door. I had no gods damned way of finding her, but I had to try.

I flung open the door and walked out, hearing Elena's harried footsteps behind me as I descended the stairs.

"It's usually Sebastian who finds her!" she called after me. "His calling card doesn't work here, but he seems able to sense her. I don't know how he does it."

Wretched devil. He had probably been right to go off on his own, but I couldn't just stand idly by. If she ended up in trouble like she had in the Bogs, she might need me. Of course, when the merrows had pulled her under, she had found *me*, and not the other way around. If she hadn't come to me on her own, she would have died that night.

Instead, she had appeared before me, shivering, her

clothing soaking wet. I had wanted to kiss her right then and there, pressing our bodies together, taking what she so willingly gave to Mistral—

I cut off my thoughts as I strode down a long hall lined with windows. I had attempted to locate the merrows after that day, but they knew better than to reveal themselves to me. Once I found them, they were dead.

"Just where do you think you're going with my daughter?"

I hesitated at the sound of an authoritative voice.

"Crap," Elena hissed, catching up to my side. "It's my father. Trust me when I say running would be a bad idea."

I stopped in my tracks and turned, my shoulders stiff. Though the king had granted me passage into his lands, I had not expected to meet him in person. I forced myself to appear calm, though everything inside me begged to continue on.

King Francis stood in an embroidered blue coat, his arms crossed, his long red hair draped across his shoulders. "I'll ask again, just where do you think you are going with my daughter?"

Eva

WE HAD FOUND a narrow deer path to walk on. It was a small blessing, because Crispin still had no idea where we were.

"You could try jumping us back," he said from behind me. "It would be a good lesson. Just envision my tower, and I'm sure you'll get us there."

"Or end up somewhere worse." I glared at a purple butterfly fluttering past my face. It had been haunting me, wanting to lick the sweat from my skin.

"You could think of Gabriel. That has worked for you before, has it not?"

I ignored him. I had shared a lot of details in the past week that I would have rather kept quiet. But if we were going to figure things out, Crispin needed to know everything. Well, *mostly* everything. Some things I was certainly not about to share, especially in front of Sebastian.

"Eva?"

"That only worked when I was drawing on someone else's magic, apparently. I was pretty charged up when I found Gabriel before."

Charged up by having sex with Mistral in an open field, but *that* was one of the details I wasn't sharing with anyone else. Especially not since the state of the Bogs was supposed to remain a secret. Sebastian knew the magic there was unstable—he had been the one to bind Mistral to the land in an attempt to control it—but the elves and other factions had no idea.

Crispin jogged to catch up to my side, a smooth

smile on his lips. "You can use my magic to bring us back."

"Nope." I walked faster. That was what had gotten us into this predicament to begin with. I had been picturing trees near the palace, not some place out in the woods I had never been before.

He caught up again, matching my pace as we continued walking. The purple butterfly was back, trying to land on my forehead. "It does not always have to be sexual. You have been using Sebastian and I to jump all over the castle for weeks."

"Unknowingly, and usually just once Sebastian pisses me off enough."

I glanced at Crispin as his expression turned thoughtful. "True. Your sexual tension with him does seem to be tied to anger."

I glared at him.

He quirked a brow in return, the soft sunlight making him look like some sort of mischievous forest god. *Follow me down this path, my dear. Nothing bad will happen.*

Yeah right. "If you're trying to make me angry, it's not going to work."

He gave me a dazzling smile, his blue eyes twinkling. "Then I suppose we should just settle in and enjoy our walk."

"If we're even going the right way."

He pointed at the sun. "It was well after noon when we jumped, so I do know roughly what direction we're heading in. Plus the moss." He ran his finger along a tree as he passed it. "It mostly grows on the north side because it enjoys the shade."

I looked up at the sun, but I still wasn't sure what direction we were going in. Of course I didn't even know what direction I was heading when I was in the city. "Okay, so we know what direction we're going in," I conceded. "But how much farther do we have to go?"

"That is indeed the question." *Although it was a question he didn't seem terribly concerned with.* "The Elven lands are not quite as expansive as the Bogs, or so I've been told, but we may be walking well into the night."

"Lovely," I huffed, my legs already tired and my mouth longing for some water. I glanced at him. If we were going to be walking for a while, I may as well get some questions answered. "How long have you suspected that I'm a conduit?"

His shrug was just as graceful as any elf's. It was hard to pinpoint exactly why, but their movements always seemed a little more fluid than anyone else's. "For a while. Your proximity to others each time you have jumped was a big clue. I was not aware that you had slept with the goblin prince shortly before your first jump though."

"You knew he," I twirled my hand in the air searching for the right word, and got a butterfly on my finger instead, "*unlocked* my magic though." I lowered my hand in front of my face, giving in to the butterfly's ministrations.

"Yes, but that's not as uncommon as you might think. Magic is a funny thing. It can react to all sorts of circumstances. Many elves come into their gifts after an intensely emotional experience. A loss, a triumph, and quite often, sex for the first time."

Having its fill, the butterfly took off and I lowered my hand. "It wasn't my first time," I grumbled. Sure, the other times had been with humans and once with a werewolf, and *nothing* that compared to being with Mistral and Gabriel... But once again, that was privileged information.

Our path faded away, and he took a moment to look at the sun and the moss, then pointed us in a new direction. "But it was your first time with an intensely magical being, as we have established. I thought that was simply the case for unlocking your magic, but with truly jumping for the first time so shortly afterward. You likely maintained some of the charge you took from Mistral."

"He said he gained magic from me too."

"Well of course," he continued like it made perfect sense. "Conduits are also amplifiers. You take the magic of others and turn it into something more. Sometimes it spills back over. The point is, now that this process has been set in motion, it will likely increase."

I thought about bringing up the odd connection I had felt, like invisible cords between us, but one of the cords had connected me to him. And I wasn't sure how I felt about that. So a change of subject it was. "And how did you come into *your* magic? Did you sleep with a queen?"

He laughed. "Hardly." He glanced at me, then turned his eyes back to the path ahead. "Do you recall the bit of my history I shared with you?"

"You mean how your mother sold you to a wizard?"

He nodded, his gaze still turned steadily ahead. "She did not sell me because I already showed magical promise. Had that been the case, she surely would have asked a higher price. I was to be little more than a servant, but the shock of such betrayal unlocked my true potential. The earth had swallowed up my family home before I knew it."

My jaw dropped. I tried to stare at him as we walked, but tripped on a stone. He grabbed my arm before I could fall, and a spark of magic flared between us.

He released my arm as if he hadn't felt it. "I didn't kill them. They were all outside, watching me being dragged away. My sisters were crying, and I was terrified. It was quite the emotional affair."

I shook my head at his words. "That's awful." He spoke as if it didn't matter, but he wasn't that old. It really hadn't been all that long ago, and that type of wound tended to last. I should know.

He shrugged. "It all worked out well enough. Once my master knew my true potential, I became like a son to him rather than a servant. He was still a harsh and cruel teacher, but he valued me, at least. Eventually he sent me to court as his envoy, where I met Queen Soraya. It was she who encouraged my research into jumping realms. She knew nothing of what King Francis explained to us. The severing of the realms happened so abruptly. She wanted to know why, and to be reunited with her consort."

"You told all of this to Elena, didn't you?"

He gave me a sheepish smile. "Yes, her involvement in this whole affair is my fault. She never even met Queen Soraya, but she is very young in her thinking, and simply wants her father to be happy."

"How is that young in thinking?"

He lifted one shoulder in a partial shrug. "To not consider the consequences, of course."

"But *you* don't consider the consequences."

His eyes were back to sparkling. "Well I'm not that much older than her, after all."

We both stopped abruptly as a cloud of darkness appeared before us. Sebastian formed from that darkness, looking entirely pissed off. "*There* you are. How in the hells did you make it all the way out here?"

For once, I was actually happy to see him. "Please tell me we are not that far."

He picked invisible lint off his white shirt, then crossed his arms. "You're far. And I searched your usual spots before venturing further. There was a messenger for you."

I glanced at Crispin, then back at Sebastian. "A messenger?"

"Yes, apparently your roommate left a message at the gates. Something about an angry nymph storming your apartment demanding to know what happened to her sister."

I winced. "Seraphina?"

"I would assume so."

I glanced around us. What a nightmare. I was doing my best to keep Braxton out of things, but I had once again brought trouble right into our living room. "Where is Gabriel? We need to get out of here."

"He and Elena were detained by the king."

Oh great, I had a feeling Gabriel was not going to be happy with that at all. "How long will it take us to make it back?"

"Long enough to have your nymph friend do something stupid."

I narrowed my eyes at the devil looking entirely out of place in the lush forest around us. "You don't care about Seraphina. You're just trying to get me to jump again."

He tilted his head. "Well as you know, I cannot carry you." He smiled.

I crossed my arms, mirroring him. "But you can give me the boost to carry myself? Is that it?"

"I could." He lifted one hand to examine his nail beds. "But I imagine Crispin would not like to be left behind. I suggest you take your boost from him."

My cheeks flushed at the very thought. "You have got to be kidding me."

Crispin gave me his most charming smile and pressed his palms together in a silent prayer to not be left behind.

I looked back and forth between them. "This is ridiculous."

"Progress takes effort, Eva," Sebastian chided.

I furrowed my brow at Crispin, still hesitant to try. We had traveled together before—I knew it was possible—but why was Sebastian pushing for it? What did he hope to learn?

Crispin turned away at the sound of approaching hooves.

All tension left me as I followed his gaze, spotting Gabriel atop a mighty buck, another one tagging along behind him.

I ran to him as he slid down, throwing myself into his arms before I could think better of it. "How did you find me?"

His eyes darkened. "I will explain later."

Okay, whatever. I glanced back at Sebastian and Crispin as they approached, though my words were for Gabriel. "We need to go. Seraphina is at my apartment bullying Braxton."

Gabriel kept a protective arm around me. "She heard of her sister? How?"

"Apparently so, and I don't know." I looked back at the other two guys again. "Are you coming?"

Something shifted slightly in Crispin's expression, but he bowed his head and approached the second buck.

Sebastian just looked irritated. "I will find you later." He lowered his chin, silently reminding me that I now had to always keep the card on me. But did the card really matter? He had found me out here too. Just like Gabriel. Finding me in the castle was one thing. We were in the middle of nowhere now. Before I could ask, he poofed away.

Frowning, I turned to the remaining two guys.

"Who is Seraphina?" Crispin asked, his expression back to normal.

"It's a long story. We'll tell you on the way."

Gabriel gripped my waist, helping me onto the larger buck before vaulting up behind me.

We had ridden together plenty of times now in the Bogs, but something felt different in the way he wrapped his arm around my waist. Something had changed today.

But what?

Gabriel

Truly, even as king Francis agreed to lend me mounts, and even as I rode into the forest, I didn't believe I could find her.

But something tugged at me, guiding the way, like an invisible cord between us. Like we were connected by more than just mutual care.

And if I was a part of this, then so were the others. And so was Eva. Only she was being pulled in four different directions.

And there was no saying which path she would ultimately choose.

13

I PAUSED with my hand on my apartment door. "You know, you really can go back to the Bogs. I'm home safe now, and I have Sebastian's card."

Gabriel's smoldering dark eyes shifted from my hand on the doorknob to my face. "Nymphs can be dangerous."

"How did you find me in the woods?"

His eyes lowered, not quite meeting my gaze. "We shall discuss that once your current crisis is out of the way."

I didn't like it, but he was probably right. One thing at a time. I had a feeling whatever he had to say, it was going to turn into a whole big conversation.

I opened the door, not sure what to expect. The first thing I noticed was that it

was eerily quiet. The second—the apartment was a

mess. The furniture was all out of place, and papers and small tchotchkes were strewn about.

The sofa was halfway across the room, Seraphina sitting on it, arms crossed and a glare locked on her face. She wore jeans and a white linen button up, her long hair skimming her tall frame.

As Gabriel stepped inside behind me, I glanced at Braxton in the kitchen with Ringo on his shoulder. Braxton had kept his hands busy with coffee, sandwich makings, a pile of freshly peeled fruit, and a bunch of shelled peanuts. He had clearly been busying himself away from the nymph for quite some time.

He gave me a *get her the hell out of here* look, nodding toward the living room.

Sorry, I mouthed, then walked past him.

Only Seraphina's eyes moved as they lifted to my face. I jumped when she finally spoke. "Explain to me how a simple delivery ended in my sister almost dying."

"How do you know about that?" I asked

Her nostrils flared. She held up one hand, letting it turn into tree bark. "I speak to the trees, Eva."

Ah, I had forgotten about that. I slowly approached the sofa to sit down. "Well if that's the case, then you also know we found her already near death."

"This must have something to do with your devil. I should never have allowed him along."

I lifted a brow, but she wouldn't have known what happened after we left the park where the trees couldn't see us. "Actually, without him she probably wouldn't have made it. He helped me find an antidote for her poison."

Her expression softened. "Poison?"

I guessed the trees hadn't seen what happened there either. "Yes, someone poisoned her, we think before she left home."

"And you sent her back there?"

I winced. "Short of kidnapping her, we couldn't really keep her away."

I jumped as Seraphina lurched forward, but it was only to bury her face in her hands, the skin now smooth and brown once more. "They won't believe her. She'll be locked away for going out without their permission, and whoever tried to hurt her will be able to do it again." She took a ragged breath and shook her head. "This was all so stupid. All for her favorite cookies."

"Cookies?"

"Yes, the packages you deliver. They are her favorite cookies."

I glanced toward my room where I had left the package, intending on returning it to her when I had the chance. "What's so dangerous about cookies?"

She moved her hands enough to slide a glare my way from between her fingers. "The danger is not the cookies, it is the contact between us. If my family knew, she would also be disowned."

"So why risk it?" I asked.

Her fingers slid back over her face. "Because we are

sisters. It was too painful to sever all contact. Now I see that it should have been so."

Braxton had come into the living room, Ringo still on his shoulder.

Ringo looked at me, then to Gabriel leaning against the wall, then down at Seraphina. "Can we get her back?"

Seraphina jumped, her hands smacking down onto her lap. She stared at Ringo, her jaw hanging open. "It speaks?"

"He's not an it," I said. "But yes, he speaks. He was there last night and he could have told you everything had you simply come in calmly enough to ask."

She looked around my trashed apartment, then shrugged apologetically. "I always check with the trees near the lake after the delivery. When they told me my sister was hurt, and a devil carried her away..." Her eyes slid to me again. "My emotions got the better of me. I apologize."

"Fair enough," I sighed. Though hopefully she was planning on staying to help us clean up. I seriously needed a nap.

"Do you have any idea who would have wanted to hurt your sister?" Braxton asked.

Seraphina hesitated. She knew Braxton, had met him a dozen times, but she still didn't trust him. I wasn't sure she fully trusted anyone. I could relate.

"She said your uncle was poisoned too," I remembered out loud. "If that helps."

She furrowed her brow. "I have twelve uncles, and not a clue who would want to harm any of them." She turned away again. "All I know is that my sister is not safe, but there is nothing I can do. I am exiled. I cannot cross into my family domain. I cannot access our well."

"I'm sorry. We never would have sent her back if we had known your parents wouldn't believe her. She seemed to think everything would be fine." I tentatively placed a hand on her shoulder. When she didn't shrug me off, I gave it a squeeze.

"I have to do something." Her voice trembled. "I have to find a way back inside, if only to pull her out."

"How were you communicating about the packages?" I asked.

She lifted her head, turning eyes shining with unshed tears my way. "With the packages themselves. I always included the next drop off where she should grow the flower, which she was to destroy before returning home."

If she only went out to get the packages once per month, it was a pretty big coincidence that she was poisoned right before she left. "What if she didn't destroy it? What if the poisoner knew she would be leaving, and used it to cover their tracks? It would look like she was attacked in the park. Even the trees said so."

Her mouth formed a little trembling *oh* of surprise. "You're right," she gasped. "The coincidence is too great. This means she was attacked because of me."

I lifted my hands in a soothing gesture before she could break down. "Let's not get too far ahead of ourselves. This is all just conjecture. First we need to figure out how to reach her before something else happens."

"*We?*" Everyone in the room but me asked at once.

I looked at each of them. "Yes *we*. She's an innocent girl. We can't just let her be killed."

I jumped as Seraphina abruptly grabbed my hand, but all she did was squeeze it. She met my eyes steadily, her tears still glittering. "Thank you."

"Don't thank me yet. I'm not sure if a nymph boundary is one I can cross."

She continued squeezing my hand. "I will tell you everything I can. Just please bring my sister back to me alive. If exile is the price she must pay, then so be it."

I looked at Gabriel, who gave me a slight nod. The nymph lands weren't in this realm. They were a near realm, sure, but they also had a boundary to keep anyone else out. Not only would I have to attempt traveling to the correct place, I would have to cross a boundary to do it. Not to mention dealing with the nymphs on the other side.

If I was going to manage it, it would take at least one of my *batteries*.

Maybe more.

14

"This is where you'll want to start." Seraphina pointed to a spot on her hand-drawn map. "You can't bypass the main entrance, but as long as you don't go near the well, you shouldn't have trouble with any of the protectors."

I looked across the coffee table at her. "Protectors?"

"They watch the well at all times. But if you go straight to Aaliyah's chamber, you can find her before anyone finds you."

I drummed my fingers on the table, not liking the sound of anyone finding me. Of course, I had to make it into their realm first.

"And she will know how to show us out?" Gabriel sat beside me. He had refused to leave for the entire discussion.

Seraphina nodded along with his words. "She will show you to the nearest portal. The one that lets out near the lake."

I barely heard her because I was looking at Gabriel. "What do you mean us?"

"You'll be using my magic to jump. I know you can take me with you. Plus, it will be good practice traveling with another."

"You sound like Sebastian," I muttered.

He frowned, but didn't take back what he'd said.

I returned my attention to Seraphina's map. The entire plan was utterly insane. My realm jumping was sketchy at best. I had proven as much just a few hours ago.

But... I couldn't just let Aaliyah get killed. It wasn't any of my business, but she was still just an innocent girl. And my long-time client's little sister.

I sat up a little straighter. I could do this. I had brought Gabriel to Mistral before, beyond a boundary. This time, I would just bring him to Aaliyah instead.

Gabriel glared before I realized someone was standing right behind me. I slowly looked over my shoulder, feeling like I was in a horror movie.

Sebastian stood behind me with his arms crossed, looking down at the map. "What exactly do you think you're doing?"

Braxton took that as his cue to get up from the couch. "I'm going to order us something to eat." He didn't so much as look at the devil as he walked past them.

I got up from the floor then moved to take Braxton's

seat next to Seraphina. " Aaliyah is in danger. We're going to rescue her."

"We already wasted a full night on that nymph." Before I could argue, he stepped forward and looked down at the map. "And how exactly do you intend to rescue her?"

"Eva is the only one who can reach her in my realm." Seraphina lifted her chin and eyed him defiantly. "I am exiled. I no longer have access. And whoever poisoned her will surely try again."

Sebastian studied the map like he would commit every line to memory. I shuddered to think what he would do if given free rein in the nymph realm. And with the Realm Breaker, he could make it there all on his own. "The bounty has been increased."

Braxton came back into the living room, an open beer in one hand. "What?"

I stared up at Sebastian, though he was still just calmly studying the map. "Yeah, what?"

"Whoever can deliver your mother will receive not only the Realm Breaker, but $500,000."

My jaw fell open.

Seraphina looked back and forth between us. "What are you talking about?"

Sebastian waved his hand, and I felt a magical bubble slide into place around just him and me. Seraphina's mouth was still moving, but I couldn't hear a word.

I looked at Sebastian. "Why add the cash? The Realm Breaker is valuable enough."

"Many would not know the true value of the blade. This will add more players to the game."

Gabriel was glaring at the invisible bubble like he wanted to punch through it. I gave him a look that said *be patient*, then turned my attention back to Sebastian again. "It doesn't really change anything."

He lowered his chin, fire flashing in his eyes. "It changes much. Word of the monetary reward will spread, and many involved already understand your connection. Soon every amateur in the city will be after you."

My gut churned. It was bad enough having vampires and fae after me. If human criminals were added to the list, I wouldn't be able to even walk the city streets without a disguise. And if they found out where I lived...

"I see you understand." Sebastian closely watched my expression. "That being said, I believe you should go forward with this rescue. The nymph realm is parallel to ours, extremely close. It will be a good test of your skills, and a test of the conclusions we reached this morning."

I glanced at Gabriel, who was still watching us, but was unable to hear us.

"But you will not use his magic. You will use mine."

My jaw fell open yet again. Once I regained control of my face, I asked, "Why?"

"Because you have already tested Gabriel's power in such a way. As we have established, your reaction to me is far different. It should be tested."

"What if I don't want to test my magic with you!"

He waited for me to calm down. I had a feeling he was counting to ten in his mind. "You plan on entering a foreign realm—a potentially hostile foreign realm—with no weapons or escape plan?"

"We're going to be sneaky," I argued. "I have no intention of going in there and attacking the nymphs."

"And what if you come into contact with the poisoner?"

He had a point, but— "Gabriel can protect me."

"While he is impressive," he said it like he didn't really think so at all, "my magic will be of greater use to you."

Dammit, too many good points. "Why are you doing this? You don't care about Aaliyah."

"That is correct, but if you can do this," he twirled one hand in the air, "it is proof that you can do more. Proof that we can finally move forward."

He was right. About everything. Double dammit. I glanced at Gabriel, though he still couldn't see us. He was not going to be happy about Sebastian going with me instead. "Fine. But no hurting anyone if we can help it."

"Of course." He gave me a truly devilish smile.

I narrowed my eyes. "Why don't I believe you?"

"I believe your roommate is in his bedroom ordering food. You may eat, if you wish, then we will get started."

I glared at him, not sure if I could eat a single bite even though I had been starving just a little while ago. Even after everything, I found that I still didn't fully trust Sebastian. I trusted him to keep me alive, sure, but just because I was useful to him. I didn't trust him to not get anyone else hurt. And that was a problem.

I almost found myself wishing I had tested things further with Crispin earlier. Surely an elven wizard would be just as good as a devil in a realm of nymphs?

I looked at Gabriel as Sebastian's bubble dissipated. Either way, Sebastian was right. Gabriel was an excellent protector, but his inherent magic was more in his physicality. This was a mission of stealth. Sebastian's shadowy magic made far more sense.

Now to explain that to the brooding goblin looking at Sebastian like he wanted to snap him in half.

)))●❊●❊●(((

"THIS REALLY IS NOT IDEAL." Crispin spun a slow circle, taking in the dark surrounding trees. Clouds blocked out most of the moon, and the city lights seemed far away in the center of the wooded park.

We were in the park where we had dropped Aaliyah off, reasoning that the closer we were to the portal, the easier it would be to end up in the right place. If only the nymphs lived behind a normal boundary. If there was a boundary I could actually see, I could easily cross it. But the portal was only visible to anyone with nymph blood.

Which was why Seraphina was with us, her eyes wary like she might be attacked at any moment. She turned those wary eyes toward Crispin. "Do not worry. There is no reason for anyone to protect this side of the portal. No one unwanted ever comes through."

Crispin stroked his chin, looking at the area Seraphina had defined as the portal. "Yes, that's not actually what I'm worried about. Our Eva usually jumps to another person. When she tries to jump to an area, things tend to go wrong."

"Can she not then just focus on my sister?" Seraphina asked.

Crispin's eyes slid toward me. "It is not just any person who can lure her."

"Stop talking about me like I'm not here," I huffed. I looked at Sebastian and Gabriel. "Can we just get this over with?"

"Gladly," Sebastian said with a smooth smile.

Gabriel glared at him while Crispin hopped into motion. I would attempt to just use Sebastian's power to guide me, bringing only him along. But this was all too new to dismiss the possible need for more of a... charge. Hence, Gabriel. And Crispin had come along to observe, and maybe to guide. Maybe he could figure something out to make this all a little easier.

As we all moved together, Ringo hopped down from

my shoulder and scampered over to Crispin, as planned. He hadn't wanted to stay behind, but there was no way I was going to risk losing him in the nymph realm. Crispin knelt, offering Ringo his hand, then lifted the little goblin onto his shoulder. The elf seemed perfectly fine with the little goblin being so close to him, which I appreciated.

Crispin pressed his palms together in front of his face, taking a moment to study each of us, including Seraphina. "Well, shall we?"

"We shall," I said, impatient to get moving. It had taken time to reach Crispin in Emerald Heights, time that Aaliyah might not have. I just hoped we weren't too late.

"Point out the portal one last time?" Crispin asked Seraphina.

Still looking nervous, she nodded, then traced a large space with her hands in the air. "It's here. I can still see it, even though its magic has been tuned against me."

Crispin tilted his head. "The nymphs can tune a boundary against a single person?"

Seraphina hesitated, then answered, "It all has to do with our magical well. My family severed my connection to the well, therefore I can no longer use the portal."

I was dying to know just what Seraphina had done to be exiled, but maybe if I saved her sister, she would finally tell me. I moved right in front of the space she had outlined, and Sebastian joined me.

I was suddenly finding it incredibly difficult to meet his eyes, so I turned to Crispin instead. "What now""

"Just like last time," he said, "but without Elena to go knocking things around."

I placed one hand on Sebastian's chest, still not meeting his eyes. I could feel the warmth of his skin, the beat of his heart, and underneath that, the dark pulse of his magic. But it didn't call to mine. Not yet.

"Dear Eva," Crispin tsked. "You know better than that."

I sighed. I did know better. I was just hoping that for once, things could be easy and not horribly embarrassing. I lifted my eyes to Sebastian's, my lips parting slightly at his expression. I had expected mocking, or irritation, but there was something else. Something that I didn't understand at all, other than the fact that it made my cheeks burn, and made my core flare with a pulse of tingling warmth.

My hand on his chest began to glow dark red and purple.

"Very good." Crispin beamed at us. "Now focus on the portal. See if you can sense it, and feel the energy of where it leads."

"I don't know how to do that." The magical glow around my hand on Sebastian dimmed with my words.

Crispin stepped closer. Ringo watched us with wide

shining eyes from his shoulder. "You know how to do this, Eva," Crispin soothed. "It's in your blood."

Sebastian waited for me to meet his eyes again before he spoke, "It's not much more than stepping across a barrier. Attune your energy to that of the adjacent realm."

"That's not what I do when I step across a barrier."

"It is, you just don't realize that's what you're doing." I opened my mouth to argue, and he sighed, his familiar irritation returning. "Just *try*, Eva."

"Fine." I stepped closer, keeping my hand pressed against his chest.

I could sense Gabriel at my back, and Seraphina beyond him. And I could sense Crispin standing even closer. And... I inhaled sharply. Maybe I *could* sense the nearby portal. It felt similar to Seraphina's energy, but undiluted.

I closed my eyes, trying to do what Sebastian had instructed. Trying to *attune* myself, though I still wasn't sure exactly what that meant.

Everything else faded away, until all I could feel was the portal, and distantly Sebastian's heartbeat beneath my palm. I wasn't sure what I was doing, but my focus seemed to be increasing the magic, which had to be what we wanted.

I hoped.

The other option was that I was just going to alert every nymph beyond the portal that someone was trying to break in.

"Um, Eva?" Crispin's tone gave me pause.

I started to pull my hand away from Sebastian, but he gripped my fingers, keeping me against him. "Just open your eyes."

I did as he asked, though I felt strange and far away, and way too in tune with the energy of the portal. I realized the space Seraphina had outlined was now glowing blue. We were lucky it was after dark, and the only things that might be in the trees around us were other magical beings. Humans knew the danger and would only come during the day.

"Can we just step through now?" I gasped.

"I think so." Crispin stepped a little closer, but didn't touch us. He looked back at Seraphina, who gave him a hesitant nod, her features rimmed with a blue glow.

Keeping my hand pressed against him, Sebastian edged us toward the portal. The magic increased, and it felt as if the very blood in my veins was glowing that same blue, matching the magical energy. Maybe that really was how I crossed boundaries—matching my energy to the realm beyond.

"Does it seem to be getting brighter?" Crispin asked.

Before I could verify his concerns, the portal swelled outward in a bright flash of light, surrounding the three of us. On instinct I grabbed Crispin's hand, then we all shifted together, leaving the park behind.

15

Sebastian and Crispin both held on to me as I lurched forward onto a smooth dirt path. Lush grass edged the dirt, swaying with an unfelt breeze. It was night here too, at least I was pretty sure it was night. High overhead, an archway of interlocking trees and vines completely sealed us in. Like Seraphina had predicted, there were no guards to greet us. Strangers never came through their portal.

Finally regaining my equilibrium, I put my hands on my hips, glaring at Crispin with Ringo still on his shoulder. "You weren't supposed to come!"

He crossed his arms and lowered his chin. "I'm not the one who made the portal explode outward to swallow us." He smiled then, looking around. "Although I do appreciate you grabbing on so I didn't get tossed somewhere else. I don't think any of us would have made it here if we weren't touching you."

Ringo scurried down from his shoulder then hopped over to me, climbing up my clothing before I could kneel to accommodate him. "We will help Aaliyah."

Dammit, he was right. Aaliyah's safety was what was important now. We needed to find her and get her out of here, or find her parents and convince them the threat of the poisoner was real. *They* had only seen their daughter after she was recovered. *I* had seen her unconscious and near death.

I looked both ways down the path. Behind us was a solid wall of wood in the area the portal should be, and in front of us was the gloomy walkway, shrouded by leaves and branches. "I guess we start walking."

"You could attempt jumping again now that we are in the realm," Sebastian suggested.

"Yeah no way. I'm not trying to travel with all four of us." I peered dubiously down the path. "Let's get moving."

Crispin made a dramatic gesture, like a fancy butler holding a door open.

I narrowed my eyes at him as I walked past. "You're not mad at all that you got pulled through, are you?"

"It's been many years since I was able to travel to another realm." He walked at my side, glancing around at the impressive archway. There were enough breaks in the upper branches to let little slivers of moonlight through, just enough to barely light our way.

Sebastian caught up to walk at my other side.

160

"According to Seraphina's map, the first dwellings should not be far. It will be simple to avoid the well, for now."

"Yes," Crispin agreed. "We are fortunate it is a small realm."

I wove closer to him to avoid a divot in the path. "You didn't even see the map."

"I did so. Sebastian has it folded up in his pocket."

"Shh," Sebastian hissed.

I stopped walking. "You stole it when we weren't looking!"

Dancing embers in his eyes were the only hint of light in the shadows where he stood. "Are you not glad to have it to guide our way?"

"Yeah, but you hid that you took it. That can only mean you want it for something nefarious."

"Or perhaps I simply knew you would accuse me of something nefarious, and did not want to deal with the inevitable argument when your little nymph may be running out of time. Like she still is now."

"Fine," I huffed. "But you better not have any ulterior motives. No harming the nymphs or tricking them into contracts."

I started walking again, anxious to find Aaliyah, and they both fell into step on either side of me.

"So what is our plan once we reach the dwellings?" Crispin strolled along, paying no mind to mine and Sebastian's argument. Of course, he was used to the arguments by now.

"According to Seraphina, Aaliyah should be in her chambers. We just have to avoid any nymphs on our way there." My eyes darted up, catching another flash of moonlight through one of the cracks. "Hopefully everyone will already be in bed. They mostly just guard their well, and we don't need to go anywhere near it."

"And if someone spots us before we can reach Aaliyah?" Crispin pressed.

I shrugged, slowing as the end of the path came into view. Soft light, maybe from candles or lanterns, cast a dull yellow glow across the ground ahead. I could hear running water and a few night insects, but no voices.

"I could create a distraction, if necessary," he whispered.

I finally *really* looked at him, not just with my eyes, but with my senses. He was absolutely abuzz with energy. "There's more magic in this realm for you to use, isn't there?"

He had confided in me before that coming to our realm was like a slap in the face. In his homeland, magic was plentiful, and he was extremely powerful. Here, he was diminished, and could no longer forge complete paths to the other realms.

His blue eyes danced with mischief. "Not as much as in Elvalanor, but far more than I've been accustomed to as of late."

I narrowed my eyes. Elvalanor was not the true name of the elven home realm, but it was one us mere humans could actually pronounce. "No magic unless

162

absolutely necessary." I turned around, my finger already lifted to point at Sebastian, but his attention was on the tunnel opening.

Without warning, he grabbed me, pressing us back into the shadows. Ringo clung to the hair at the nape of my neck, shivering against my skin. Reacting more quickly than I ever could, Crispin pressed himself against the opposite side of the tunnel.

Whispering voices came near, and we all fell silent to listen.

"We are running out of time."

"No one suspects a thing. We can still make this work."

"Not with so many drawing from the well."

The voices faded as they walked past.

I turned toward Sebastian. "Can you follow them?"

"Why?"

I rolled my eyes. "Because they sound super suspicious. They might be the ones who poisoned Aaliyah."

"Fine." He gave me a quick irritated look, then disappeared in a cloud of darkness. I wasn't sure if his magic was increased here too, but as long as he was as good as he was on earth, he would be fine.

The rest of us, however—I looked at Crispin. "Let's go. We still need to find Aaliyah."

We crept toward the edge of the tunnel, but it was too narrow for us to see much of the surroundings beyond. "Can you scout ahead a little bit?" I asked Ringo. He was the size of a small animal, and there were probably plenty of those scurrying about in a realm of nymphs. In the darkness, he should be fine.

I knelt as he scurried down my arm, lowering him to the ground to scamper out of sight.

"Wow," Crispin said softly. "And here I had assumed the little guy was completely useless."

I glared at him. "That little guy has saved my life. Or at least saved me from being kidnapped."

"How?"

I smirked. "Sharp teeth. He is also extremely handy for eavesdropping. And all he wants in return are various forms of potatoes."

Ringo scampered back into sight and we both crouched in front of him for his report. He looked beyond excited to be helping out. "Lanterns in the direction of the dwellings. A few nymphs milling about the walkways, but if we stay in darkness, we can probably avoid them."

"Perfect." I held my hand out for him, lifting him back to my shoulder.

"Turn right out of the entrance and walk close to the trees," Ringo's little voice chittered in my ear.

I led the way, peeking my head out before following with my body. I did as Ringo instructed, keeping my back pressed against the trees forming the tunnel. I could see what he was talking about now, and where the light was coming from. The residences were small and dome shaped, placed in large circles around walkways lit by torches. I could see a much larger dome beyond, and knew that's where the well resided, according to Seraphina. There were some woods and rivers beyond that, but that was the extent of it. Nymphs usually resided in our own realm, but created pocket realms for safe dwellings. The realms always centered around the well, the source of their power and clan connection.

We crept along, keeping to the tree line. I knew Aaliyah's room wasn't in the first set of residences, but the one beyond, closer to the well.

I froze at the sound of a door opening, and a tall male nymph emerged from the nearest dwelling. He was close enough for me to watch his profile as his brow furrowed, then his head started to turn our way.

Crispin yanked me to the ground. I felt a flutter of his magic as the grass grew a little taller around us, completely concealing our hunched forms.

My heart thundered in my throat as we waited, then I heard the soft sound of footsteps walking away from us. I waited another minute before I let my breath whoosh out of me. "Nice going," I whispered.

Crispin parted the grass enough to peer outward, then stood and offered me his hand.

I took it, even though he would know how much I was shaking. I *really* didn't want to do battle with nymphs just to get Aaliyah to safety.

Crispin stepped close, his eyes watching our surroundings. "Are you alright? You can go back to the tunnel if you need to. I can try finding her on my own."

I swallowed the lump in my throat and shook my head. "No. She doesn't know who you are."

"Fair point." With the coast entirely clear, he looked at me. "I just don't like seeing you afraid. You weren't so fearful when we faced the fae."

I managed a small smile. "I was working on pure adrenaline then. Somehow sneaking around is far more terrifying."

He squeezed my hand. "Just follow my lead. The magic here flows through me easily. I can conceal us again if needed."

He kept hold of my hand as he started leading us further along. Eventually we had to leave the tree line of the tunnel, veering around the back of several domes toward the cluster where Aaliyah would be located.

It occurred to me that had I just allowed myself to trust Sebastian, I could have sent him straight to Aaliyah to convince her to come with us. It would have been easy enough for him to find her with the map, and he could just poof right back to the start of the tunnel if anything happened.

But I hadn't trusted him. If it was more convenient to sacrifice someone, I didn't trust him not to do just that. I just didn't know enough about his motives to think otherwise.

Crispin and I crouched back down in the grass as we studied the next circle of homes. Small, oval panes of glass were the only windows, and most of them radiated with light. It wasn't late enough for everyone to be asleep.

"It should be that one," I whispered, pointing to one of the homes. I nudged Ringo with the side of my face. "Do you think you can go peek through that window to see if she's in there."

Without answering he hopped down from my shoulder, then scurried through the grass, entirely concealed.

I watched his dark shape as it hopped up onto the small ledge bordering the pane of glass. He peered in for a moment, then dropped back down.

A moment later, he crawled back onto my shoulder. "She's in there!"

A voice cleared behind us, and my heart fell to my feet.

"And just what do you think you're doing peering through my daughter's window?"

⁘⁘

CRISPIN and I stood shoulder to shoulder before a tall male nymph with Seraphina's strong jaw and sharp eyes. He wore a white robe, almost like a toga, contrasting with his blue tinted skin. Though Seraphina took after his appearance, I would guess his magic was more akin to Aaliyah's. Water instead of earth.

Behind us were four more nymphs with honest to

goodness swords pointed at our backs. One of them held Ringo by the scruff of his neck.

We had been led to one of the larger domes, lit by smooth glass lanterns. I imagined it was usually a meeting hall, or a place to gather for meals, but now it had turned into a courtroom.

I winced as a blade nudged my back. "Speak, human."

Either they couldn't sense my celestial blood, or they didn't care to try. "I already told you." I aimed my pleading eyes at the male nymph, Fiorus. "Your daughter is in danger. If you just bring her here, she can tell you what happened."

It felt like his sharp eyes were trying to bore holes through my skull. "My daughter risked the dangers of the city, and she paid the price. She was lucky to make it back to us. You have no business here." His eyes narrowed. "Though first I must know how you came to be here. *Only* our people can pass through the portal."

I wasn't sure if it would be helpful to point out that his words obviously weren't true, since we had indeed come through the portal. Probably not. "Her uncle, your *brother*, was poisoned too. Surely you can entertain the idea that the same happened to Aaliyah." I actually wasn't sure if it was his brother or her mother's brother, but I figured my odds were fifty-fifty, so I took a shot.

Fiorus' nostrils flared. "He went out into the city and was cursed because of it. *Not* poisoned."

My eyebrows shot up at that. I had thought Aaliyah

was just being childish when she thought her uncle was cursed. "We gave her a poison antidote and it cured her. It wouldn't have cured a curse."

"She was not poisoned," he snapped.

"If I may—" Crispin started to step forward, but a blade lifted to his throat. He went stiff, then stepped back into line with me. "Perhaps your daughter should be the one to explain what happened."

"There is no need to explain what we already know." Those intense eyes turned back to me. "Now tell me how you came into our realm."

I almost told him, but if that was all he wanted from us, would he kill us once he knew? The blade at my back felt very sharp and very real. If we got out of this alive, I might have a slice in my jacket to show for it.

"Your daughter is in danger," I said again. "Once I know she'll be safe, then I'll tell you how we got here."

"She is safe within her home." He strode closer, trailing his white toga around his strong body. He was a good head taller when he came to stand right before me, and he had to lean forward to put us eye to eye. "And I will not be fooled into believing you care for her safety."

I swallowed audibly. With a sword at my back and an imposing nymph in my face, I was not a happy camper. I didn't want to give away Seraphina and Aaliyah's connection, but keeping their secret wouldn't do much good if we were all dead. Well, everyone but Seraphina. She was relatively safe on the other side of the portal.

Everyone jumped as a cloud of darkness burst into life near me, quickly forming into Sebastian. All the blades instantly pointed his way, but he was looking at Fiorus.

It only took Fiorus a few seconds to recover from his shock, then his eyes went wide with fury. "What is the meaning—"

Sebastian calmly extended a rolled parchment his way, giving no acknowledgment to the swords practically slicing his shirt. "This will explain everything."

Fiorus hesitated, then took the parchment, his outraged expression melting into confusion as he unrolled it and started reading.

I shifted nervously, my palms sweating as we waited for a reaction. I had no idea what the parchment might say, but at least with Sebastian here I might stand some chance of not getting stabbed. He could at the very least create a distraction for the rest of us to get to the portal. Though I would need to figure out how to snatch Ringo back first.

Fiorus finally lowered the parchment. "This isn't possible."

Sebastian stepped closer to me, and all the swords followed him. "I assure you it is."

I slid my eyes toward him, hoping for some sort of explanation, but his attention remained on Fiorus.

Fiorus lifted the paper, glancing hesitantly at the guards, then back at Sebastian. He lowered his voice. "Where did you get this?"

If I had someone looking at me that intensely, I would have flinched, but Sebastian merely smiled. "Perhaps you'd like to speak of this privately."

"I do not even know who you are. Why would I speak with *you* about this?" He encompassed me and Crispin in his attention. "*Any* of you."

"If we were not here to help," Sebastian said, "I could have taken that parchment *elsewhere*."

The parchment crinkled in Fiorus' hand.

I glanced at Crispin, but it was clear he also had absolutely no idea what was going on.

"Fine." Fiorus' eyes lifted to the guards. "Leave us."

The guards hesitated, their swords lowering just a fraction. And I couldn't blame them, I was entirely baffled too. He was actually going to speak with all of us unguarded? Including a devil who could poof in at will?

But at his glare, the guards obeyed. The one with Ringo dropped him lightly on the ground, then followed the others. As they left the dome and shut the door, I could hear them muttering amongst themselves. They didn't go any farther than that.

Fiorus looked at each of us. "They are gone. Now speak."

"Everything Eva has told you is true," Sebastian said. "She is a bleeding heart and came here with the intention of saving your daughter from the poisoner."

"Hey—"

Sebastian rolled his eyes to me. "Do you truly wish to argue?"

I crossed my arms and pouted. "I guess not. But wanting to save a young girl doesn't make me a bleeding heart. It just means I'm not an *asshole*."

Sebastian smirked. "Either way, it has led us to something far more interesting. Fiorus' brother was not cursed, he was poisoned by a devil." He turned his smirk toward the nymph. "At the behest of Fiorus himself."

The room went so silent we could have heard a pin drop. Instead, we just heard Ringo's claws on the floor as he tiptoed over to me.

I expected some form of denial, but Fiorus simply shook his head, "Who else knows?"

"At least two of your people," Sebastian replied. "They found that parchment in your chambers."

Fiorus visibly paled. "Where are they now?"

"I have detained them."

"Why would you help me?"

That was exactly the question I wanted to know. Sebastian didn't help *anyone* for free.

"I want the name of the devil you hired."

My brows lifted. By the gods, I had so many questions.

"Fine," Fiorus huffed. "But I want to know how you came to be in my realm."

Sebastian looked bored. "Eva can explain that if she wishes."

I stepped forward. "Just wait a minute. We are

ignoring one big problem. Your daughter is still in danger. And you *knew* she was actually poisoned."

He bared his teeth at me, and I thought he was going to tell me to get the hell out, but at a look from Sebastian, his expression sobered. "The poison would not have killed her. She was safe in that park with the trees."

I lifted a hand. "Wait a minute. You *knew* she was in the park. You knew she—" I cut myself off as the rest fell into place.

"He knew she was receiving packages from Seraphina," Sebastian finished for me. "He had her poisoned, but not enough to kill her. If his own daughter was *cursed*, he would avoid any suspicion for killing his own brother. Just as he would teach her a lesson for disobeying him, making her too fearful to leave the realm again."

Crispin's jaw fell open. "Wow. That's dark."

Fiorus completely crumpled the parchment in his clenched fist. "You know nothing of this. I have done what is best for my daughter."

"By poisoning her?" Crispin reiterated.

Sebastian seemed to be getting a real kick out of everyone's reactions. His eyes danced with unexpressed laughter.

I shook my head. And here I thought my family dynamic was messed up. "So Aaliyah's not in danger then. Other than having an asshat for a father."

"Correct," Sebastian said. "We had no real need to come here."

I wasn't so sure about that, but I kept my mouth shut. I would open it later to tell Seraphina she should get her sister out of here. She was better off being exiled.

"She *is* in danger," Fiorus said abruptly.

We all turned to look at him.

He glared at each of us. "I don't know who you are or why you would care to protect my daughter, but if that is still your aim, then I need your help."

I stared at him, hardly believing his words.

This evening had just been *full* of surprises.

16

"Are we sure we want to involve ourselves in this?" Crispin whispered as four guards escorted us back toward the portal.

I had no good answer for him. Turned out, Fiorus had made a deal with a devil to "curse" his brother, because his brother was going to try killing him first as a result of a power struggle over the nymph's magical well. He wasn't able to tell us what he had given the devil in exchange—secrecy on that front was part of the contract—but he was able to tell us that he'd gotten what he wanted. Only, his other brothers had grown suspicious. And so the devil had poisoned his daughter too. No one would ever suspect he would go so far to avoid suspicion.

I knew I was still having trouble believing it.

As we reached the end of the long, spooky path, I glanced at Sebastian. He had gotten what he wanted too

—the devil's name. And I knew why he wanted it. There were few devils in the city, and the news that one had delivered my mother's orders to Lucas... chances were high it was the same one. Find the devil, and maybe we would find my mother.

One of the nymphs cleared his throat. There were three men and one woman, all dressed in a similar white toga style. Their different coloring hinted at a few forms of elemental magic.

Nervous, I returned my attention to the blank wall of wood where the portal should be. I would need to reactivate it to get us out of here.

When I didn't do anything, the nymph cleared his throat again.

Sighing, Sebastian grabbed my hand and placed it on his chest.

Crispin did the same, only a little more gently and far less rudely. He gave me an encouraging smile.

Ringo shifted on my shoulder, clinging tightly to the collar of my coat as he prepared himself for the shift.

I took a deep breath. I could do this. It hadn't been *that* hard the first time, and this time we were going back home. I didn't need to attune my energy to the nymph realm. I just needed to focus on how home normally felt.

Both men's hearts beat steadily beneath my palms. I could feel their magic. Sebastian's, dark and unnatural. And Crispin's like a clear flowing river and crisp green leaves. And even though he wasn't there, I thought of

Gabriel. His magic like woodsmoke and deep earth. And Mistral's like night air and ozone.

The portal flashed to life, steady this time, not reaching out to grab us. Each of them keeping hold of one of my hands, the guys walked me into the light. For a moment everything was blinding blue, then we lurched forward, our feet crunching on dirt.

Seraphina ran to us as soon as the portal winked out. Gabriel followed just behind her.

"What happened!" She snatched my hand out of Crispin's, pulling me toward her. "Where is my sister?"

I winced. Seraphina was not going to like what we had to tell her. "Let's go get a drink and we'll explain everything."

"I don't want a drink," she hissed. "I want my sister here with me, safe."

I looked at Gabriel beyond her. "Trust me, she's safe enough for now, and you're going to want a drink after everything we have to tell you."

Her expression softened. She looked at each of us, then finally nodded her assent.

Gabriel gave me a knowing look. A look that said, *Just what trouble have you gotten us into now?*

⟩ ⁑ ⁎ ⁕ ⁕ ⁑ ⟨

GABRIEL'S HORSE awaited us just inside the iron gates to the Bogs. After we had explained things to

Seraphina, I had convinced Sebastian and Crispin I would be safe for the night.

Well, convinced was a rather strong term. I was pretty sure Sebastian had watched us the entire way, but whatever. My head was a little spinny from a few drinks, and I had gotten what I wanted. Or, what I *thought* I wanted. Now that I was faced with an evening alone with my two goblins, or three if you included Ringo, I was nervous despite the drinks.

But I had to face things sooner or later.

Shutting the gates behind us, Gabriel boosted me onto his horse.

I slid forward, making room for him as I tangled my fingers in the horse's soft mane. "Has she been waiting here for you the entire time?" He had been with me since the previous day, and now it was probably just a few hours from sunrise. It seemed a long time to wait.

He climbed up behind me, settling me back against his chest with one arm around my waist. "She is a goblin horse. She knows when to wait for me."

I shook my head as he turned the horse around and we started off toward the Citadel. "Now wait a minute, I might have had a few drinks, but I'm still sober enough to know that doesn't make any sense."

"A dog will wait at the door for its owner not at the first sound of their arrival, but as soon as the owner has the intention to go home. How is this any different?"

I glanced back at him. "Do dogs really do that?"

He simply smiled. "Are you ready?"

Man, what a loaded question. "Are you ready, Ringo?"

His paws knotted in my hair, just like I was doing to the horse's mane. Before either of us could say anything else, Gabriel nudged his horse into a gallop. I settled in to his warmth, watching the dark trees streaking past. Everything seemed calm, serene even. But I knew it wasn't quite the case. The wild goblin magic was unraveling.

I just hoped nothing had happened while we'd been gone.

17

I SAT in a cushioned chair near the fire, a full glass of floral goblin wine in hand. The heat melted into my tired bones, and the wine was enough to make me feel like I might doze off at any minute. Ringo had already done just that at the dinner table, his belly full of roasted potatoes.

Now, why had I been so reluctant to come here?

Oh yeah, the goblin watching me from the other chair with his storm grey eyes and otherworldly beauty. His white hair fell long across the shoulders of his charcoal shirt. I knew the shirt was buttery soft, but not as good as the smooth skin underneath.

One corner of his mouth ticked up. He had a glass of wine too, but hadn't yet sipped it. "What are you thinking about?"

I frowned. No way I was telling him my actual

thoughts, but we had a bargain of truth between us, so there would be no lying. "Wouldn't you like to know?"

He leaned forward in his seat. "I would, very much.

"

He had taken all the news in stride, as was his way. Sebastian was often irritated, and Gabriel had a temper. Crispin was calculating. But Mistral? The waves always just seemed to part around him. Even with his realm in danger, and his own life at stake, he sat there watching me perfectly calm, waiting to see what I would do.

Gabriel had left us to take a shower, and our silence had been comfortable, until now.

Now, for some reason I found myself blushing. "What do you think of Fiorus' plan?"

He crossed one ankle over one knee, leaning back in his seat. "I think it was wise of him to snatch the opportunity for outside help. He's in over his head."

I shrugged one shoulder. "Yeah, that's if he's telling the truth about everything."

"He was desperate enough to poison his own daughter. I believe the danger he faces is very real."

And that danger was his own family. Even after all the things I had thought of my mother, it was still difficult for me to wrap my mind around it all. Currently, Fiorus was the patriarch of their clan. He controlled their magical well, and made the rules. But his brother, the one he'd had poisoned, had hatched a plan with several others to overthrow him. It would have meant Fiorus' death, and the nymphs taking over part of the city for themselves. They didn't want to stay stuck in a pocket realm anymore. They wanted their own true realm, with a boundary like the goblins, elves, fae, and angelics.

But that would require moving their well, and risking everything.

Mistral finally sipped his wine, still watching me. "You wonder if it's the right thing to do—aiding Fiorus."

"Well he *did* poison his own daughter."

"But that's not why you're questioning things."

I narrowed my eyes. "I had almost forgotten how annoyingly perceptive you are."

"I prefer *charmingly* perceptive."

I smirked. "Sure. If that's your preference."

He leaned forward again, and my breath caught as he stroked a finger between my brows. "I prefer to know just what is causing that little worried crease right there."

I scowled. "I do *not* have a crease right there. And what isn't there to be worried about? The increase on the bounty? Your unstable realm? Involving myself in nymph politics I know nothing about just to acquire the name of a certain devil?" Sebastian had acted like he didn't recognize the name, but I had a feeling he would already be on the case while I sat by the fire and sipped wine.

His smile remained entirely serene. "You believe people should be free."

"Of course I do, I—" I shut my mouth, realizing that

was exactly what was bothering me about the Fiorus thing. He wanted Sebastian to return to his realm, to spy and ferret out any other nymphs plotting against him. And to do that, Sebastian needed me to bring him across.

It was Fiorus' own business what he would do to those who opposed him, but the real issue was, I thought they were right. I thought if they wanted to have their own boundary and be a part of the city, then they should be allowed to do just that.

Only, that would take the well and the pocket realm away from everyone who wished to stay behind. So maybe there were no right answers.

Mistral stood and offered me his hand.

I looked up at him, suddenly nervous.

"I know something that might relax your nerves."

"I'll just bet you do."

He rolled his eyes playfully. "Not like that. Of course, I'll gladly keep that option open."

I slid my hand into his and magic prickled across my skin. I reacted to all of the guys, but Mistral... It was like he embodied the pure wild magic of the land. It was simply what he was, and what it had taken to unleash my own power.

I kept my wine glass in my free hand as he helped me stand, but instead of leading me from the room, he pulled me close. His cheek brushed mine as he slid light kisses down my neck. His soft hair smelled like lavender and vanilla.

"What are you doing?" My voice was breathy, his kisses sending tingles from my neck to between my legs.

"Keeping the options open," he breathed against my skin.

When I didn't move away, he pulled back just enough to claim my lips. His tongue slid into my mouth and I molded my body against him, holding my wine glass awkwardly out to one side.

Never breaking the kiss, he deftly took it from me and set it on a small table, then his hands were massaging my lower back. A moan escaped me, and he took it as an invitation to delve deeper.

I reached for the waist of his pants, and he broke the kiss. The heat between us made his eyes go from stormy to almost silver. "I still have something to show you, Eva."

"I thought that's what was happening." I smiled.

"*That*, we will continue as well."

He took my hand again, this time actually leading me away from our seats. I grabbed my wine at the last moment, then allowed him to guide me from the room.

I wasn't sure what he could show me that would be more exciting than taking his clothes off in front of the fire, but as long as I could have both, he could lead me into an ice cold river and I wouldn't care.

WELL, it wasn't an ice cold river. Steam swirled across the surface of the natural spring, bordered by lush green grass and the stone pillars surrounding the courtyard. The stars were giving way to dawn overhead, but I couldn't see the rising sun with the stone walls surrounding us.

I stepped toward the water's edge. "Now I see what you meant about relaxing."

Mistral came up behind me, his hands sliding down my shoulders to my upper arms. I had left my jacket back by the fire, and just his skin against my bare arms made my mind return to what we had started. "Would you like to go in?"

I looked at the surrounding stone walls. There were several windows, too high for me to see into.

He leaned his cheek near mine, pressing his chest against my back. "I swear to you if anyone sees us, I will know immediately." He didn't bring up the fact that plenty of his people had seen us in the nearby village when it had been overrun by vines, and I appreciated that. Despite that incident, I was still entitled to a little modesty.

And if he said no one would see us now, I knew it was the truth. I stepped away from him just enough to tug my shirt over my head, then I started unbuttoning my jeans. I glanced back at him as he watched me. "You're coming in too, right?"

He inclined his head. "Gladly," he hesitated, his eyes going distant, "but Gabriel is now searching for us.

I believe he might find *you* before he would even find me."

That hit a little too close to home with Gabriel having found me in the elven forest. We still hadn't had a chance to talk about it, and I had almost forgotten with everything else going on. "How do you know he's coming?"

Mistral's gaze refocused on mine. I am bound to the land, and to the stones of the Citadel. They speak to me, in a way."

I didn't have time to ask more questions as Gabriel walked through the nearest stone archway.

A few droplets of water had soaked into his white T-shirt from his damp hair. His hair, while already pure black, held highlights of blue and purple in the early morning light. Now that he had found us, he just stood there watching, unsure if he was welcome.

Mistral looked over at me.

I crossed my arms underneath my lacy bra. "You planned this."

"That is not true. I would love some time alone with you, but... I leave this choice to you."

My throat was suddenly dry at the idea of both of them in the hot spring with me. Oh gods, what had I gotten myself into?

And why was the idea suddenly all I could think about, my entire body tight with need.

"Fine," I said, pretending I was put out even though he knew I wasn't. I turned my back on him, removing my boots and jeans and tossing them aside. The bra and panties went next, and I refused to look back to see what was happening as I stepped into the water.

Heat closed around my legs and I nearly groaned it felt so good. Mistral was right, it was exactly what my tired body needed. Smooth stones lined the pool, creating steps into the deeper water. I was in up to my waist when I finally heard a small splash behind me, drawing my eye.

Steam rose around Mistral, clinging to his gray skin before swirling up and dissipating in the air. Gabriel had stepped in behind him, and even though the second man was much larger, they were both a sight to behold. Mistral slender and tall, muscled but lithe, his skin and hair ethereal. And Gabriel, powerful, earthy—and looking at me like he wanted to devour me from the top down.

Mistral reached me first, taking my hand to guide me into the deeper water, now reflecting the purple and pink hues of dawn. The water reached my shoulders, pulling tendrils of my brown hair to float around me.

Mistral deftly moved my hair, cradling my back against his chest as he kissed my neck.

I closed my eyes, overwhelmed with the sensation along with my nerves about the entire situation. The connection I felt with both of them terrified me, and I wished I could read their minds. I wished I could know if it felt the same for them.

I had told Gabriel that it was my magic that had

chosen them, but he had been right. The choice had been mine, or maybe fate. Maybe it was fate that tugged the invisible strings between us.

I hadn't heard Gabriel move, but I somehow knew he was now standing in front of me. I opened my eyes. He watched me with heat in his expression, but even after everything, he was still waiting for an invitation. I knew if I reached out to him, that would be it. That first time, I had been trying to save his life, and after that trying to keep the wild goblin magic from consuming us.

But there was no danger now. No excuses. If I gave in to what I wanted, there would be no hiding it anymore. Magic couldn't be blamed. I would have to fully admit that it was *my* choice.

There was a flicker of hesitation in Gabriel's eyes, and I sensed what it might feel like to just let him walk away. My heart ached at the very thought. I could sense Mistral waiting on bated breath behind me.

I lifted one hand from the water, and held it out toward Gabriel.

His expression shifted, and I knew even after everything, he was surprised. He was still surprised that I was choosing him. His powerful body slid through the water, his exposed chest gleaming with condensation. It dripped in sparkling rivulets down toward the little trail of hair leading lower.

He took my hand, raising it to his lips, grazing my skin with a reverent kiss. His eyes remained locked with mine, even as Mistral's hands skimmed my waist from behind, hugging me until he cupped my breasts.

My nipples hardened at his touch. I realized we had moved deep enough into the water that my feet were barely touching. I was sandwiched between them, both of them tall enough to have their shoulders above the water. I had a moment of panic being so deep in a spring where wild magic surely bubbled beneath the surface, then Gabriel lifted me by the waist and kissed me.

I wrapped my legs around him, suddenly safe and secure, feeling the hard length of him pressed against me.

I didn't want to say anything to ruin the moment, almost as much as I didn't want to admit my plans for being with them again. But I also didn't want this moment to end. I broke the kiss, and panted, "I'm on contraception now."

Gabriel's eyes widened for a moment, then he smiled, pulling my mouth back toward his. His tongue delved between my lips, tilting my head back. Mistral chose that moment to come up behind me again, his lips sliding across the side of my neck, every kiss tugging an invisible string that traveled right between my legs.

Magic danced around us, warm like the sun for Gabriel, and twinkling like stars for Mistral. I had a thought about the moonlight glow for Crispin, and Sebastian's auroras, but I pushed it all away.

Our hearts seemed to beat as one, pulsing along

with the wild magic. The water around us was almost too hot. Steam and sweat gathered at my hairline, dripping down.

As if already sensing my discomfort, Gabriel walked us toward the edge of the pool, then leaned my back against the cool grass. I could see the sun overhead now, but only for a moment as he dove between my legs, holding me just above the water so that my lower back and part of my legs were still warm.

Goosebumps prickled the rest of my wet skin as the steam dissipated around me, then Mistral was there, claiming my mouth just as Gabriel's tongue plunged into me. I groaned into Mistral's mouth, and just as before, the feeling of both of their hands on me was almost too much.

Mistral moved to my breasts, sucking one into his mouth until it was almost painful.

"Yes," I breathed, and he sucked harder as Gabriel licked shivering lines between my legs, building me toward climax. The little stars around us changed, glowing more warmly than before just as the orgasm hit me.

Delicious pulses of electricity coursed through my body and I could no longer tell if I was cold or hot, nervous or just excited for more. Whatever it was, I could *feel* both of them. I could feel those invisible cords connecting us, tenuous and shining gold.

I looked down across Mistral's body. Even with the cold air, he was still hard and ready, his skin slick with steam. Gabriel helped me as I slid a little more into the water. Mistral was always so in control, guiding me, guiding *us*, and now I wanted to give him what he had given me. I wanted him to let go and trust.

He watched me with heat in his eyes as I slid my mouth over his shaft. Even just that first touch gave me exactly what I wanted. He threw his head back, his hands fisting the grass.

Gabriel came up behind me, kneading my hips with his fingers, a silent request. I wiggled my hips, and a moment later I felt him at my entrance.

I was suddenly reminded of just how big he was as he slid in oh so slowly, careful not to hurt me. I pressed my mouth around Mistral as far as I could go, then slid back, slowly finding my rhythm. The sounds reverberating from his chest spurred me on. He might be an ancient, cunning goblin prince, but for me, he was letting down his guard.

With one last thrust Gabriel filled me completely, and I groaned around Mistral's shaft. He reached his hands down, knotting his fingers in my hair. Not guiding my mouth, but making it clear he wished for me to stay there.

But it wasn't his hands in my hair nor Gabriel at my hips that bound us together. I could feel those cords even stronger now, like shimmering threads of gold. They didn't just bind me to Mistral, and Gabriel to me. They went through all three of us.

Gabriel started thrusting into me with abandon,

building a second wave of warmth between my legs. I fell into the same rhythm with Mistral, matching Gabriel's pace. Even in the growing sunlight I could still see the glittering stars and warm glow of magic around us, pulsing with every thrust.

Gabriel cried out as he came, and the feeling of him inside me with no protection between us sent me over the edge. Mistral came into my mouth a moment later with Gabriel slumping lightly over my back, keeping the three of us together.

When I could breathe again, I blinked at the stars in my vision. But there was something else. Something strange. I lifted my head as much as I was able. "I can hear both your heartbeats. And I can feel them, like they're in my own chest." My words were so soft I wondered if they had even heard them.

Gabriel kissed the middle of my back. "I feel it too."

Something touched my arm, and I knew it wasn't Gabriel with his hands at my waist, nor was it Mistral with one hand in my hair and the other stroking across my shoulder blade.

I tilted my head to the side as a flowering vine curled up beside me. It turned a soft white flower my way, almost as if it was an eye looking at me. I knew I should probably be scared— the wild goblin magic was unpredictable—but something about it felt safe, like I could sense exactly what state it was in. It felt... content.

Gabriel slowly pulled me back into the water with

him. He wrapped his arms around me protectively. "What's happening?" He looked past me at Mistral.

Mistral lowered a finger to the little white bloom, lightly stroking across its petals. His striking eyes lifted to mine. "Do you feel it?"

Though he was being vague, I knew exactly what he was asking. I nodded.

"It's the bond between us."

Once again, I knew exactly what he was saying, because I could *feel* it. For better or worse, Mistral was bound to the land. And now with that golden cord between us—

It called to me too.

18

WHEN I WOKE UP, only Gabriel was in the bed with me. I had my back to him, but the heavy arm around my waist let me know who it was. Or I supposed that wasn't really true. I would have known it was him with my eyes closed, without him speaking a single word. I wasn't sure where Mistral had gone. He never seemed to sleep much.

Gabriel shifted at some small movement I must have made. His arm lifted, stroking a lock of hair back from my face.

"That's how you found me in the woods," I said. "The cord connecting us. I felt it in Crispin's tower, then again last night. Why didn't you want to talk about it?"

"I worried it might make you pull away," his voice rumbled against my back.

I supposed it was a valid concern, given how I had

been acting. I turned over, pulling the sheets up over my nakedness and re-situating myself on my pillow to face him. Normally I would have gotten dressed at the spring, but I hadn't protested when Gabriel scooped me up and carried me all the way to Mistral's bedroom for round two.

"It's confusing. But it doesn't bother me."

He gave me an all too knowing look.

"Okay, it doesn't bother me *yet*."

"And does last night bother you?"

I laughed. "Oh, not in the slightest, though I had hoped Mistral would be here too when I woke up. I should probably be off to find Sebastian soon. He should have found information on our mysterious devil by now."

"And what about the nymphs?"

I shrugged one shoulder. "Sebastian made a deal with Fiorus. I'll take him back to their realm, and he can do what needs doing."

I still wasn't sure what to think about it. Seraphina was livid about Fiorus poisoning Aaliyah, but she was still hesitant about pulling her out into exile. Of course, if Fiorus' opposers won, Aaliyah could live in the city and still be connected to the well. I had a feeling that was what the younger nymph would prefer, minus the demise of her father.

Gabriel moved a finger down the crease in my brow.

I frowned at him.

"It is an unfortunate circumstance, but I think we

need to focus on the bounty. Lowly human criminals may not take the elf king's protection seriously."

I lowered my eyes. I had been trying really hard to not think about *that*. "They may not even know about the protection order. Word circulated through the magical community, not through the entire city."

His hand went back around my waist, giving me a light squeeze until I looked at him. "You opened a portal to another realm last night. If Sebastian can find this other devil and discover where your mother is located, you can reach her."

"Maybe. If she's in a near realm. A *really* near realm."

"If she was unreachable in a far realm, the bounty would not exist. And without the Realm Breaker, she cannot escape to one. Not since the pathways were destroyed."

He was right. She had to be in a near realm. And ever since Dawn had told me about the female devil, I was wondering if she was actually in the hells. Maybe once I left the Bogs, Sebastian would already have an answer. We could move forward.

The door opened seemingly of its own volition, and Mistral came in carrying a massive silver tray with coffee cups, a carafe, and the biggest stack of waffles I had ever seen. Fresh cut strawberries and a bowl of fluffy whipped cream were next to the waffles.

I salivated at the sight of the food, coffee, and the goblin in a fresh white linen shirt, unbuttoned to show the upper portion of his chest. Even though we'd only gone to bed a few hours ago, I was imagining undoing the rest of those buttons one by one. And that whipped cream—

Gods, what was wrong with me? It was breakfast time. I was supposed to be hungry, not *thirsty*.

Mistral gave me a knowing smile, then approached the bed with his tray. Gabriel sat up to take it from him, not at all bothered by his present state of nudity. Myself, I was looking around for my clothes, but I didn't see them anywhere.

"They got a little wet," Mistral said, reading my expression. "But the sun will have them dry soon enough."

Frowning, I tugged the sheet up around me, awkwardly reaching for the coffee.

Gabriel poured it for me, giving me a look that said I was being silly, then reached for the only cup of tea on the tray.

"Hey, I'm half human, and I was raised entirely human. We don't just go walking around naked all the time."

"Were you not raised in part by werewolves?" Mistral asked playfully.

I rolled my eyes. "Yeah, but they only get naked when they shift forms."

The door that Mistral had left partially ajar creaked open a little further. I heard the sound of little paws scuffing on stone, then Ringo hopped up next to the impressive waffle stack. He licked his chops, then deflated a little as he realized how close behind him Mistral was.

Momentarily giving up on the waffles, he hopped over to me. Also oblivious to my nudity, he crawled onto the sheets covering my lap. He turned wide eyes toward my face. "The forest is noisy today. Lots of chatter. Something happened last night."

I could tell he was proud to have brought me the news, not realizing that *we* were what happened last night—or, early this morning, actually. "Lots of chatter?" I asked innocently, glancing over his head at the other two goblins.

He nodded, not noticing my nervous glance. "The land got really loud, then suddenly very quiet. Now everyone is talking about it."

I wasn't sure who *everyone* was. Maybe he meant the tiny goblins that would lurk on stone ledges throughout the Citadel. "You tell me if they say anything else, okay?"

He nodded excitedly, then glanced back at the waffles.

"Go ahead," I laughed.

Gabriel frowned as Ringo hopped over to the waffles and took one off the top of the pile with his little paws.

Mistral just seemed to find it all terribly amusing. He walked around the bed, then sat a little behind me so I could lean my back against his chest. My nerves instantly quieted.

He leaned forward, grazing my cheek with his. "You should eat. I believe the land will remain silent today. Gabriel can accompany you home without worry." He lowered his voice, though everyone would still hear. "Though I do wish I could go with you."

I pulled away enough to look at him. "Do you really?" He always seemed so unfazed by things. I wasn't sure how much he truly cared to be involved.

"Of course. Not only to join in your adventures, but —" He looked past me at Gabriel. "It is lonely here, sometimes."

The pair exchanged a look that I would probably never understand. It was clear they both knew each other better than anyone else.

Clearing his throat to break the tension, Gabriel fixed a plate with three waffles piled high with strawberries and whipped cream, then handed it to me.

I looked down at the plate. "Do you really think I'm going to eat all of that?"

He smirked. "I thought you might have worked up an appetite. You know, when the land got all loud then quiet."

I snatched the plate before he could say anything more in front of Ringo. Even though the little goblin was far older than I was, he was still rather childlike. I didn't want to give him any nightmares.

Mistral waited for my reaction as I cut into the

pancakes, making sure I had a plump slice of strawberry and a dollop of whipped cream on my first bite. I chewed, then nearly died right then and there. "Gods, that's good. Why is everything you guys make so incredible?"

Chuckling, Mistral reached around me for his cup of coffee. "Trust me, Eva. It's the least we can do."

⁙ ⦁ ⦁ ⦁ ⦁ ⦁ ⦁ ⦁⦁

No FAE or devils accosted us on the way home, and that included Sebastian. I had expected him to be waiting outside the gates when we arrived, but he was nowhere to be seen. The sky above us was gloomy and gray, but I was in relatively high spirits despite everything.

Not having to deal with Sebastian was just a bonus.

"I smell troll," Gabriel said as we ascended the steps to my apartment.

"Troll?" Ringo gasped into my ear.

I furrowed my brow. Dawn was the only troll-blooded person I knew, but I hadn't expected her return so soon. *And* I would have expected a call from Braxton the moment she arrived. He had never really enjoyed Dawn's company, and I couldn't blame him. She was an acquired taste.

We reached the landing and I put my key in the door, but it was already unlocked. Bracing myself, I opened it and went inside. Sure enough, Dawn was sitting on the sofa, a new periwinkle cup in hand.

There was another on the low coffee table, presumably for me.

As we walked past the kitchen and into the living room, Dawn's eyes started with Gabriel's feet, tracing a slow lingering line all the way up to his face. "So sad that he has a shirt on this time," she said wistfully.

I rolled my eyes as I approached the sofa. "I thought you liked *elves*."

She leaned forward, picking up the other cup and handing it to me as I sat. "I might have a crush, but I can still appreciate fine artwork, Eva."

Braxton came out of his room at the sound of our voices. He walked toward the kitchen. "Don't hate me, Eva. She wanted to see who you would come home with if you didn't have any warning."

Of course she did. "You know, you don't have to do what she says."

He opened the fridge, taking out a carton of milk. "Hey, she paid me twenty bucks."

"I will wait in your bedroom," Gabriel sighed, clearly tired of the conversation.

As soon as my bedroom door was open, Ringo made a run for it. Drinking straight out of the carton, Braxton returned to his room, and suddenly Dawn and I were alone.

I took a sip of the fresh latte. I'd had plenty of coffee, but damn, those gargoyles could really brew a nice cup. "I have my friend looking into Rian, if that's why you're here."

Dawn angled her impressively long legs toward mine. Her pantsuit today was a saturated dark purple. She looked great in jewel tones, and she knew it. "How long will that take?"

I shrugged. "Not long, but I'll let you know." I studied her expression, from her small smile to the glint in her dark eyes. "You've learned something new."

Her smile kicked up a notch, and she nodded.

"And you're trying to figure out what you can get from me in return." I didn't say it like it was a question.

She smiled broad enough to show her perfect white teeth. "Yes, that was my intention, but my curiosity is getting the better of me. Tell me what you were doing all night with your very large, very handsome goblin, and I'll give you my information for free."

I glared at her. "If I have to tell you something in exchange, then it's not free."

"But it's also not terribly expensive, especially given what I've learned."

I glanced at my closed bedroom door, then shook my head in defeat. "We're... seeing each other."

"Well *obviously*. I'll need a little more than that."

"Fine," I huffed. "We're sleeping together."

"And what about the high goblin of the Citadel?" She asked slyly.

My mouth gaped and I almost spilled my coffee. "How do you even know about that!"

Her eyes sparkled. "So it's true then. Honestly, when my goblin contacts mentioned it, I thought they had to be mistaken. My little Eva, dating not just one goblin, but two?"

I glared at her. "It's complicated."

"I'm sure it is," she laughed. "And that look on your face is worth far more than anything else I could have gotten out of you." She leaned forward. "Now would you like to hear the little tidbit I brought for you?"

"Yes," I grumbled, lifting my coffee for another sip.

She sipped her coffee too, her eyes still shining with laughter. "I've been tipping heavily at Lapis Brews," she lifted her cup, "and in exchange the gargoyles have been speaking more freely around me. Word is, the angelic Lucas is on a warpath."

I sputtered on my coffee. Gods, not Lucas. After not running into him for the past week, I'd been hoping he'd finally given up on interfering with my search for my mom.

Dawn lifted a brow. "Interesting. You've gone two shades paler just at the mention of his name."

"Just tell me what you know."

She wrinkled her nose at my tone, but continued, "He believes he's been betrayed. Someone called in a favor, presenting him with one of his feathers, but now he believes the feather was stolen. The favor he was doing wasn't for the person he thought."

"His feather?" I asked.

"Yes, something else I learned from the gargoyles. When an angelic owes someone a debt, they will give that person one of the feathers from their wings. When that person would like to settle their debt, they present the feather."

So had my mom had a feather? But if the favor called in wasn't actually from her, that would mean— "Who does he think someone tricked him?"

Dawn shrugged. "The gargoyles weren't sure, they just knew that he was hunting someone, and that was why."

So that's where he had been, hunting whoever had actually tasked him with killing night runners. But that same person had also asked him to protect me... And then there was Marcie, the celestial woman who was working with him, who had tried to warn me away from the guys...

Just what in the hells was going on?

We both turned at the sound of voices outside my front door proceeding a knock. Recognizing the voices, I called out, "Come in!"

The door opened, and in walked Elena and Crispin, clearly already deep in their own conversation. They stopped talking as they realized I wasn't the only one in the room, then Elena's face lit up.

"Is this your old boss?" She approached the sofa, nearly tripping over her own brown boots. Along with the boots she wore torn jeans, a striped tank top, and a jean jacket. "What perfect timing. I spoke to Rian this morning."

Dawn gave me a horrified expression. "Just how many people have you told?"

"Not that many!" I promised. "But she had to know enough to ask around."

"And *she* is?" Dawn asked tersely.

Elena did a little bow. "Princess Millelena, at your service."

Crispin rolled his eyes at Elena as he moved to sit beside me on the sofa. "She's Eva's old boss, not a queen from a neighboring kingdom." He straightened his moss-green shirt, which somehow matched his tweed trousers, then put a companionable arm around my shoulders.

I wiggled a bit at a tickle of magic between us. I was enjoying seeing Dawn with her jaw agape at a total loss for words, but when she looked back and forth between the three of us, her eyes lingered on Crispin's arm around me.

Seeming to finally realize what he had done, he withdrew it.

"*Anyways*," Elena drew out the word as she slunk forward, then sat cross legged on the floor. "Rian is single *and* he's intrigued. He remembered you, and said he would like to meet for tea."

Dawn lifted a hand to her chest. I thought she might pass out then and there. "He—wait. He wants to meet me? He wants... tea?"

Grinning, Elena nodded.

I couldn't help but match her grin. Honestly, I hadn't expected this outcome. A lot of the older elves weren't really interested in outsiders, especially outsiders with troll blood.

Dawn tore her eyes from Elena, then looked at me. "Eva... What do I do?"

I had absolutely never seen her like this, and I had to admit, it made me feel a little sentimental toward her. I gave her an encouraging smile. "You go to tea."

She lifted her forgotten coffee cup, but didn't drink. It seemed more like she was just lifting it out of reflex. "I go to tea," she repeated.

I nodded. "And if you get any more information from the gargoyles, you give it to your beloved Eva for free."

Crispin watched the exchange with an amused expression before lightly placing a hand on my shoulder and leaning toward my ear. "When you have a moment, I need to speak with you. Alone."

His tone was far more serious than I had ever heard it. And just like that, the lighthearted moment was broken.

19

ELENA AND CRISPIN must have spoken beforehand, because the princess slid easily into her role of distracting Dawn while Crispin and I retreated to my bedroom. Ringo was curled up on my bookshelf, and near him stood Gabriel, perusing the few titles. Most of them were from my teenage years, and they weren't exactly fine literature. I was ashamed to admit I had fallen out of the habit of reading once I reached adulthood.

Crispin shut the door behind us, then whirled on me. "What in the hells were you doing in the wee hours of the morning?"

I wrinkled my brow, glancing at Gabriel, then back at Crispin. "Didn't you want to speak alone?"

"Oh he can stay." He waved a dismissive hand toward Gabriel. "I have a feeling he had something to do with it."

"Wait a minute—" The pieces of what he was saying clicked together in my mind. "Early this morning. You mean you felt—" I wasn't quite sure how to finish the sentence.

"I felt a surge of magic," he said. "And something else." His eyes flicked toward Gabriel. "Please just tell me what you were doing so I can make sense of it."

My face was already burning just at the thought of explaining it to him. "I'd really rather not."

Gabriel stepped away from the bookshelf toward Crispin. "You feel the connection too, don't you." He didn't say it like it was a question. "You weren't just checking the apartment to see if Eva was home. You knew she would be here."

Oh boy, this was not good. Or was it? I couldn't tell. I was entirely out of my depth. "Crispin, what *exactly* did you feel?"

He pushed his blond hair out of his face, and I found myself watching the muscles of his forearm, bare beneath the rolled up sleeve of his shirt. He gripped his hair for a moment as he shook his head, then lowered his hand. "I felt a surge of completely wild magic, and when I opened my eyes, there were tiny stars floating around me."

My shoulders slumped with relief. "Oh thank the gods, for a moment I was wondering if you had felt—" I bit my lip, glancing at Gabriel.

Realization widened Crispin's blue eyes. "Oh, good goddess, you two were—"

I shifted my feet and cleared my throat, glancing at Gabriel again. "*Three*, actually."

His brows lifted. "Sebastian?"

"No!" we said in unison.

"No," I said again more calmly. "Mistral."

He pursed his lips, thinking. "Well that explains the surge of wild magic, I suppose. His connection to the Bogs would naturally bring that out, though I'm not sure how it was sent down the connection between you and I."

"Okay about this connection," I looked back and forth between the two of them. "Where did it even come from?"

"Oh, I don't fully understand what it is," Crispin laughed, making Gabriel frown. "It's fascinating though, isn't it?"

"Something like that," I grumbled. My next thought made me wince. "So if you felt... everything, does that mean Sebastian felt it too?"

"I'd say it's likely." He glanced around the room like the devil in question might be hiding in the closet or behind my curtains. "Where is he, anyway? It's rare for him to not be by your side nowadays."

"I actually don't know." I pulled Sebastian's card out of my back pocket, then stepped toward Crispin. "I expected to see him already. He was supposed to let us know what he found out about the other devil."

I rubbed my thumb across the surface of the card, focusing my thoughts on Sebastian. I wasn't exactly eager to see him, especially not knowing that he had probably sensed what I'd done with Mistral and Gabriel, but I did want to find out what he'd learned.

Crispin leaned toward me, observing the card. "Is something supposed to be happening?"

"Yeah," I flipped the card over, perplexed. "That's usually all I need to do to summon him."

Gabriel had moved closer, his attention also on the card.

I rubbed it again, and nothing happened.

"Well," Crispin muttered. "This certainly does not bode well."

Given all that had occurred, it was a vast under-statement.

)) ⁕ ❀ ❀ ❀ ❀ ⁕ ((

DAWN LEFT with a promise from Elena to set up her tea date with Rian.

As soon as she was gone, Braxton had come back out of his room. He sat on the sofa, a slice of leftover cold pizza in his hand. He had changed into a white T-shirt and gray sweatpants, comfortable on his night off from any mercenary work "Are you sure you *want* to find him? You could just, you know, let him be gone."

I swiped a palm across my face, shaking my head as I leaned back against the sofa cushions. "He was finding information on the devil who delivered my mother's message. Or maybe it wasn't my mother's message.

Either way, it was the devil who called in a favor from Lucas."

"And we learned all this from gargoyles..." Braxton trailed off, clearly skeptical.

"I think Dawn's information is good. It lines up with everything."

Crispin perched on the arm of the sofa beyond Braxton. "But we do not know for sure that this is the same devil involved with Fiorus."

"There aren't a lot of devils in the city," I argued. "Let alone female ones."

Elena's eyes followed each of us as we spoke. "Isn't it weird though that Sebastian didn't already know about her?"

"Unless he was lying." Gabriel leaned against the wall with his arms crossed.

I reached for the open box of cold pizza on the coffee table. "He didn't even have to lie. We didn't question him directly. When he said nothing, I assumed he didn't know her."

"Then we shouldn't worry about him being gone."

I looked up at him. "Like it or not, he's a part of this. I would have never gotten this far without him."

He glowered, unable to argue.

"Perhaps Fiorus would have further insight," Crispin suggested.

Elena sat up a little straighter. "Oh, are we going to the nymph realm? Can I come this time?"

"No," we all said in unison, including Braxton.

She hunched her shoulders and pouted. "Fine. But I did get your boss a date. I should get to have at least a little fun."

I rolled my eyes. "None of this is fun, but fine. You can come with, but not to the nymph realm."

"Then where?"

I looked at each of them. "Dawn said Lucas was on a war path because he thought he had been betrayed. And if this female devil was the one who brought my mom's alleged message, she'll be the one he's after."

"Eva, no—" Gabriel pushed away from the wall.

I stayed seated, cold pizza in hand. "You know it's our best option."

"What's our best option?" Elena was practically bouncing with excitement.

"To go to the Silver Quarter and find Lucas. If he thinks he was betrayed, he's no longer going to care about me. And if he wants to find the female devil," I shrugged, "he probably has a much better idea of where she is than any of us do."

"He tried to kill you," Gabriel grumbled.

I shrugged again. "Who hasn't?"

Gabriel gave me a dark look, obviously not seeing the humor.

Only Braxton smirked. When my humor was too dark, he always still laughed.

Because what were best friends for?

20

WHILE I STILL THOUGHT GOING TO the Silver Quarter was our best bet, Gabriel had convinced me to at least visit a few gargoyles and see if they knew how to reach Lucas first. Then there was also the Circus. That was where I had first met him, and also where he had tried to abduct me. I wasn't sure what other business an angelic would have at the carnival/casino, but he did seem to frequent the place. We still hadn't heard from Sebastian, and I had done everything short of setting his card on fire.

Elena looked up at the sign for Lapis Brews, the periwinkle sign with deep blue lettering matching their enchanted cups. "Coffee? There's nothing exciting about coffee."

"I beg to differ." I reached for the door.

Even though we were heading into evening, the

place was packed, standing room only. I squeezed into the crowd, looking for the end of the line.

Elena and the guys filtered in after me. Even Braxton had come along, with Ringo riding on his shoulder for a better view than I could afford. The best view would be with Gabriel, but he was waiting out on the street, keeping an eye on things.

I grabbed Elena's hand so she wouldn't get lost and pushed a little closer to the counter. A female gargoyle, her skin a stony, dappled charcoal, worked the register, taking orders and flashing smiles. Her bat-like wings were tucked close to her back, protruding above the scoop neck of her blue tank top.

Two male gargoyles made the orders as the female took them, their periwinkle aprons looking tiny and out of place on their huge frames. They were both even bigger than Gabriel. I had a feeling the counters had been built specially to accommodate them.

"A far different crowd than the Dark District," Elena commented, pushing close against my side.

And she was right. It was a cashmere sweater and diamond jewelry type of crowd, though mostly magical. A few humans braved the line, but not many. Even if you weren't intimidated by the gargoyles, the rest of the crowd was a lot to take in.

Braxton's chest bumped into my back. I didn't see Crispin anywhere.

"We might have been better off at the Circus." The

closeness of Braxton's voice startled me since I hadn't realized he had leaned forward.

"You're probably right." But what I wasn't saying out loud was that I was hesitant to take Elena there. I was under her dad's protection. I really didn't need to piss him off.

Eventually we reached the counter, and the female gargoyle flashed us the same smile she had given everyone else. I wondered if her face ever got tired, or if it was easier to hold an expression when your skin could turn to actual stone.

"I'll take your honey and rose latte with oatmilk." I'd had plenty of time to look at the menu while we waited.

The gargoyle shifted her smiling face to Elena.

"Citrus and tomato vine cappuccino please." Elena beamed at the gargoyle, her earlier disappointment over visiting the coffee shop long since forgotten.

Braxton ordered a run of the mill hot chocolate, then backed up a little as planned, giving us space from the next people in line, who would probably be pissed when we didn't immediately step aside.

I leaned forward across the counter, lowering my voice. "I'm also looking for the angelic, Lucas. I need to talk to him. It's important."

The gargoyle's smile wilted. "You know we don't all know each other just because we have wings."

"Really?" I asked. "Because I'm pretty sure you were all talking about him just the other day." Maybe they hadn't been the ones working when Dawn had gotten her information, but I was guessing at least one of them had, and both male gargoyles stilled at my words.

Her dark eyes narrowed. "You know him?"

"Far too well."

She glanced back at the two guys, one of whom was already looking at her. She nodded for him to take her place at the register, then gestured for us to walk further down the counter to where people picked up their orders.

Elena and Braxton both followed.

"Look," the gargoyle braced her elbows on the counter, "I don't know who you are, but you better not tell Lucas we were talking about him. It *won't* end well for you."

Gods, I already had half the city after me. I did not need to get on the bad side of the gargoyles. "Hey, I just want to talk to him. Point me in the right direction and I'll never bring it up again."

She studied my face like she was trying to decide whether or not she could believe me. When another customer stepped too close, she glared at him until he stepped away. "Fine. I don't know where he is right this moment, but I heard he's been going to the Dark District lately. A place called," she furrowed her stony brow, "something about kisses. I don't remember. The vampires always have such silly names for things."

"Crimson Kisses?"

She snapped her fingers. "Yeah, that's it." The fingers she had just snapped shifted to point at me. "But you don't tell him I told you."

"I won't tell him a thing."

"Good." She half turned as one of the male gargoyles brought our order. She took the three periwinkle cups, then set them on the counter in front of us.

"We didn't pay yet," I said.

"Don't worry about it." She smirked. "If you have dealings with Lucas, this is probably the last *blessing* you'll ever get." She turned away and sauntered back toward the register, giving her wings a little flick behind her.

Elena reached for the cup with her order scribbled on it. "Well she was... charming."

I handed Braxton his cup, observing his lowered brow.

"Do I need to remind you what happened last time we went to the Dark District?"

I started shuffling through the crowd toward the door. "Oh come on, getting chased by a pack of vampires was *so* not the worst thing that happened to us."

"I was talking about me being held hostage," he grumbled.

Crispin found us just as we reached the door. He looked forlornly at our coffee cups. "You already ordered?"

I shifted my coffee to my left hand as I went for the door. "Yeah, where were you?"

He took the door from me to hold it open. "I saw a woman with an antique enchanted amulet. I had to know more."

"Of course you did." I walked outside to find Gabriel waiting for us, and realized maybe I should have ordered something for him.

I gave him an abashed look, then offered him my coffee, even though I knew he preferred tea.

Smiling, he put an arm around my shoulders instead and started us walking. "Where are we going next?"

"Ever been to the Dark District?"

"It always comes back to the vampires, doesn't it?"

"It would seem so."

But at least Ivan was dead, and the head vampire of the city, Elizabeta, was allied with King Francis. Going to the Dark District shouldn't be a problem.

"She didn't offer *me* her coffee," Crispin muttered behind us.

"That will teach you for being too curious for your own good." Elena said haughtily.

"That's the pot calling the kettle black," Crispin argued.

"*Elves*," Braxton sighed.

I grinned at Gabriel, and he was already smiling back at me. But I didn't miss how he kept part of his attention on our surroundings, always looking for threats, and my smile fell. If something bad had happened to Sebastian...

Well, it would take a pretty big *threat* to take out a devil. A threat I would focus all of my attention on, ignoring the gnawing feeling at the pit of my stomach, hinting at how I might actually feel if he were truly gone.

21

"YE-AH," Braxton drew out the word as he looked up at the red lipped sign for Crimson Kisses, "we aren't going to stand out at all." He glanced at Gabriel in his casual street clothes, then at Crispin looking like he just stepped out of some vintage English pub, then at Elena in her striped shirt, jacket, and jeans.

"Don't worry about it." Elena patted his arm. "I know the management."

I gave Ringo a reassuring shoulder bob as we all stood on the sidewalk in the Dark District—just after dark. Perfect timing for all of the younger vampires to come out. The older ones usually didn't show up until around midnight.

"And *that's* why you got to come along," I said, hoping Elena's father would never find out about it.

He hadn't been pleased when he had learned his daughter posed undercover at a vampire bar as a bartender. He would be even less pleased if he knew I took her back to the establishment. But as she had said, she knew the management, including Lilith. If Lucas had been coming around here, they would be the ones to ask.

Gabriel stepped closer to me as a pair of female vampires swept past us, one holding the door for the other as they entered the bar. They both looked pale and a little bit sleepy, and would surely be finding willing victims amongst the humans who frequented the Dark District.

The allure for humans was lost on me. I personally would not enjoy being treated like a *pet*.

With the two female vamps out of the way, Braxton held the door open for us, giving me a pointed look.

I had offered to let him stay home, but he claimed he would never forgive himself if he stayed back and I got eaten.

We all went inside. Candles already dripped across tall tables lining the far wall. There were some lower tables in the middle of the floor, bordered by the artfully carved bar. It really was a beautiful space, minus the vampires now watching us with hunger in their eyes.

Ignoring them, I led the way to the bar. For once, I probably wouldn't be the first on the menu. Two elves, a goblin, and werewolf would all be more tasty than little old me. Vampires couldn't steal power from blood, but the more powerful blood did give an extra kick.

I slid onto one of the barstools. Elena remained

standing at my side, smoothing her hands across the bar in a proprietary fashion.

I raised a brow at her. "Miss your old job?"

Her eyes sparkled with mischief. "Sometimes. I really wasn't here for long, but it was nice to be treated like something *other* than a princess."

"Just what did your father think you were doing while you were here?"

She smirked. "He didn't think anything. I know how to get beyond the gates without him noticing."

"Yes," Crispin confirmed, squishing in beside her. "Something he has grilled me on during numerous occasions."

"And that's why I've never told you how I do it." She lifted her nose in the air.

Despite everything, and despite where we were, I couldn't help my smile. Elves were pretty to look at, but I never would have thought I would enjoy their company so much. It almost made me reluctant to achieve our purpose. Once I found my mom and whoever had created the bounty, we wouldn't all have much of a reason to hang out all the time. It made me sad to think about it.

Not that it would stop me from finding my mother.

Someone finally came out of the back room to tend to the bar, and unfortunately it wasn't Lilith. I didn't know her well, but she had known my mom once upon a time. I had a feeling she was quietly rooting for me, and if she knew anything about how to find Lucas, or what he had been doing in the Dark District, she would tell me.

The male vampire glided up to the bar, recognition sliding through his eyes upon seeing Elena. "Girl, you are so lucky Ivan is dead. Wouldn't be smart for you to show your face around here otherwise." His hair was gelled into dyed black spikes, his eyes a pale blue.

Elena winced. "Yeah, sorry for lying about who I am."

He laughed, grinning wide enough to show fangs as he tugged at the collar of his black button up. His eyes flicked to Ringo on my shoulder, but he didn't comment. "Don't apologize. Things get dull after a few hundred years." He leaned forward and lowered his voice. "Now I can say I worked with an undercover elven princess." He straightened and returned his voice to a normal volume as he looked at the rest of us. "Who are your friends?"

He must not have been here the night I came with Braxton, or the night I came to *rescue* Braxton.

Elena crooked a finger at him, bringing him closer again so she could whisper in his ear. He was mighty close to her neck, but he behaved himself, his expression giving absolutely nothing away of what she was saying. The older vampires were like that with their expressions. I was surprised more of them didn't play poker, but maybe gambling lost its appeal after a few centuries.

When he finally pulled away, he looked at each of us, including an extra long look for Gabriel, who had taken the barstool on my other side. "The guy you're looking for has come in a few times asking for Lilith. She's been avoiding him because she thinks it's funny."

Vampires. The humor was probably the most baffling part of their behavior.

"Do you know what he wants with her?" I asked, my own theories already running through my mind. Lilith knew my mom, and that meant she might also know Marcie. Had *she* been the one to manipulate Lucas, or was she just as much in the dark?

"Not a clue." He shrugged. "Not a nice guy though. Has an evil glint in his eye."

"Will Lilith be in tonight?" Elena asked.

"Sure," the vamp said. "Though not until midnight. You're going to have to wait a while."

"Do you need any help behind the bar?" Elena asked, surprising me.

The vamp's brow lifted. "Of course. Tips were double when you were around." He walked away to help another customer with a little swish of his slender hips.

We all looked at Elena.

She shrugged. "What? We have to wait anyway, and you have no idea how much people like to talk to bartenders. I may even have the information we need long before Lilith comes in for the night."

"Bravo, princess." Crispin shooed her away so he could have enough room to slip onto the barstool where she'd been standing.

I watched Elena walk behind the bar like she owned the place, Sebastian's card feeling like a heavy weight in my back pocket. He *never* went a full day without pestering me. Something was definitely wrong. Maybe I could go to him. Maybe I could use Gabriel and Crispin's power, then just picture Sebastian—but I had no idea where we would end up. Or where *I* would end up. There was no guarantee both guys would come with me.

And... did I really owe Sebastian a rescue? He had rescued me multiple times, sure, but he had ulterior motives. It wasn't *me* he cared about.

My watch buzzed, and I half expected it to be Sebastian, though he had never actually called me. I looked at the screen and saw a number I recognized.

"I'm going to the bathroom," I told the guys.

The other option was the street, but I could already hear it getting loud out there. Almost as loud as it was starting to get in the bar. I slid from the stool, already knowing Gabriel would be following me to wait outside the door.

Once I was alone in a stall with a loudly buzzing electric light overhead, I answered the call.

"Eva?" Seraphina's voice was strained. I could hear shouting somewhere near her.

"Yeah, it's me. What happened?"

"They did it. They took the well out of our realm. It's here in the park. It's utter chaos."

My heart skipped a beat. "What! Fiorus was under

the impression that they were still just plotting. Sebastian was going to—"

"Whatever my father wanted with your devil is moot. The well is here now, in the middle of the city. Everyone is fighting."

I hated to ask, but, "Why are you there?"

She huffed loudly into the phone. "The well is the power source of my entire clan. Of course I felt it as soon as it became available to me once more. But that's not important. These idiots have made my clan vulnerable and now everyone is in danger. I need you to come here and help us return the well to where it belongs."

"Um, I have no idea how to do that."

"Then your devil. Bring him. Surely he can figure something out."

"He's missing."

"Eva!" she hissed.

"Okay, okay, I'll be there as soon as I can."

She hung up before I could, and I just stood in the bathroom for a moment, letting my mind catch up. So much for waiting for Lilith.

⁞ ⁞ ◉ ◉ ◉ ◉ ⁞ ⁞

GABRIEL and I stepped out into the street. Crispin and Braxton had agreed to stay behind with Elena. She could gather her information bartending, and speak with Lilith when she arrived. And if she didn't, Ringo was scampering around listening for any dirt he might dig up. I trusted Braxton to look after him.

Laughing couples strode past us dressed in black lace and crimson velvet. Most of them were human, but when in the Dark District, a particular level of flair was expected.

"What do you plan once we reach the park?" Gabriel glared at a pair of young guys coming a little too close, swerving and already drunk, and they quickly gave us space.

"I don't know." I started walking, wondering if we would be lucky enough to catch a cab. "Calm Seraphina down, I guess. I might be able to help hold their portal open, but I sure as hell can't move some giant magical—"

Arms clamped around my torso so abruptly that my breath shot out of me. In a heartbeat my feet were off the ground. Gabriel spun to grab me, but I was already airborne. I watched helplessly as he was lost to the street lights below.

"What are you doing here?" Lucas' words were nearly lost to the rushing wind and the massive beat of feathered wings.

"Looking for you, you psycho!" I rasped, then clamped my jaw shut after having the realization that he might not care about me staying alive anymore.

He flew us through the dark night, his arms like iron bars around my ribs, bruising as I couldn't help but kick my feet below me. It didn't seem to bother him, and he flew effortlessly higher until we reached the flat top of a building that had to be about twenty stories high.

He unceremoniously tossed me onto the concrete, then landed gracefully beside me.

Groaning, I half rolled over to look up at him. "What in the hells is your problem?"

He stalked around me, blond hair fluttering in the wind, his great feathered wings flicking with irritation. "The missive I received was *not* from your mother." He turned to pace in the other direction, flicking his wings again.

I managed to sit up, wincing at the bruises that would already be forming under my jeans from the fall. "Yeah, I know. That's why I was trying to find you. I heard you were after the devil who tricked you."

He spun on me, fury widening his eyes. "She did not *trick* me. She somehow came into possession of the feather I had given your mother."

I wasn't about to point out that that was exactly how she had *tricked* him. "Do you know who she is? The devil?"

"I do not. And now Marcie evades me as well. I believe she was involved in the whole scheme." He stopped pacing to stand directly over me. "But why would she care about keeping you alive?"

I was once again slapped in the face by the thought that Lucas would no longer care if I lived or died, and we were *very* high up. "That's what I'm trying to find out. This has to have something to do with the bounty, but why trick—um, convince you to kill night runners, and then to protect me?"

He narrowed his eyes at me for a long moment. Long enough for my pulse to nearly choke me. But then finally, he turned away to continue pacing, the wind gusting his white feathers. "That is the question, isn't it?" He whirled on me again. "Where is Sebastian?"

It felt weird sharing information with an unpredictable crazy person, but he was looking for the female devil too. Exactly what Sebastian had been doing before he disappeared.

I explained as much.

His eyes widened again, this time with realization. "He would know her, of course."

"He didn't say that he knew her. He just went to find out more about her."

"All devils know each other."

Yeah, maybe I should have thought of that too. "She was involved with some nymphs. She made a contract with their leader. Do you know why?" Lucas definitely wasn't on my side, but at least one of us needed to find this other devil. And probably kill her. Lucas was far better suited to that than me.

He waved me off. "She would want their well, of course. Devils only search for power. They make contracts for power. Wells are an incredible source of raw magic. That's why they must keep them in other realms."

I digested his words. We might be going entirely

down the wrong path, but could a coincidence this big ever really be a coincidence?

I swallowed the lump in my throat. "The well isn't in another realm anymore. It's in the middle of a park in the lower city."

He went perfectly still. "How long has it been there?"

"I don't know. Not very long."

His feral smile sent a chill down my spine. "Get up."

"Why?"

"You want to find this other devil, do you not?"

I stood, not because he had ordered me to do so, but because I was finally feeling steady enough. "Well yeah, I guess."

"If the well is in this realm, that is where she will be. With you as a token, she will have to give me the truth."

I took a step back, but since it placed me closer to the edge of the roof, it wasn't really an improvement. "A token?"

"She wants you alive." He looked me up and down. "For *some* reason. I will dangle what she wants before her, and she will choose if it is worth the truth."

Before I could argue, he dove toward me, clamping his arms around me again. Seconds later, we were airborne, and this time I couldn't quite stifle my scream.

22

THE NEXT TIME Lucas tossed me to the ground, it was a relief to land on grass damp with evening dew. I skidded across it, toppling against a tree that still wasn't as hard as the building's roof had been.

"Eva!" Aaliyah hurried toward me and started helping me to my feet as Lucas touched down gracefully beside me. She gave him an appropriately frightened look, then muttered, "Where have you been?"

I didn't have time to explain it to her as Fiorus spotted me and marched in my direction, his white toga floating around him in a way so perilous that I hoped he was wearing underwear.

"You! You were supposed to prevent this from happening." He gestured back toward a small copse of trees surrounding a massive iron cauldron glowing with blue light.

I winced. "I'm guessing that's your well?"

He reached me, his anger so intense that I started to step back, but then Lucas was there, his hand around Fiorus' throat, lifting him up enough that his sandaled feet barely touched the grass. "Where is the devil?" Lucas said evenly.

Fiorus sputtered, unable to speak. Aaliyah gripped my arm, trembling. I didn't see Seraphina anywhere.

Lucas tossed Fiorus onto the grass like he weighed nothing.

The other man slowly sat up, rubbing his throat and looking up at Lucas with a mixture of malice and undisguised awe. "I don't know where he is," he rasped. "He was supposed to stop this from happening. We had a contract!"

Lucas loomed over him. "Not *that* devil. The female."

Fiorus' brow creased, his eyes shifting to Aaliyah still clutching my arm. We hadn't been allowed to see her—to tell her what really happened.

"Never mind," Lucas growled. He looked at the well, and I had a feeling he was speaking more to himself than to any of us when he said, "She'll come for it. All we have to do is wait."

Fiorus got to his feet, giving Lucas a wide berth as he edged toward me. At least he didn't seem angry at me anymore. "I must return the well to our realm. It's not safe here."

I observed the giant cauldron skeptically. "How did

anyone move it to begin with? It has to weigh a thousand pounds."

"It was shifted from our realm to this one, just like walking through a portal," Fiorus explained.

More nymphs had gathered around, muttering amongst themselves and watching us, but especially watching Lucas glaring at the well like it had personally affronted him. I had a feeling those who had shifted the well were yet to reveal themselves. They were all just acting confused.

"Can't you just shift it back?" I asked.

Fiorus swiped a palm across his face, shaking his head as he did so. "I don't know how it was moved to begin with. It should have taken a great gathering..." He waved a hand in the air. "Ritual!" He whirled on me. "And you were supposed to stop this from happening!"

I took a step away, bumping into Aaliyah. "Hey, your contract was with Sebastian. I was just going to bring him back to your realm, but now I can't find him anywhere."

Fiorus' eyes darkened. "Then he betrayed us."

I wasn't sure which *us* he was talking about. Surely not him and me. "I think this has something to do with the female devil you originally had the contract with."

He didn't seem to know what to do with my calm response. "I gave him the name, but I never saw her after she finished her task."

I was dying to know what he had given her in exchange, but he had already sworn up and down that

243

the contract would not allow him to divulge that information. So I asked another question instead. "Did she ever see the well?"

His spine straightened abruptly. "Of course not."

Lucas had gotten closer to the magical cauldron. A few brave nymphs stood in his way, but it was clear they were already wavering. Fiorus turned and marched toward them, though what he would do when he reached them was anyone's guess.

I turned toward Aaliyah. "Where is your sister? I came because she called."

Aaliyah's eyes shone with unshed tears. She hardly looked any better than the last time I'd seen her. "Father threw her out of the park. It was terrible. She gave me this and told me to call you again if you didn't show up." She held up Seraphina's phone.

"Can you tell me what happened with a little more detail than your father was willing to provide?"

She lowered the phone and hunched her bony shoulders, huddled in her long white dress. "I don't even know. I was in bed, and the next thing I knew I was here. When the well got shifted out of our realm, it was like it pulled us all with it."

I didn't want to break it to her that their realm might not even exist any longer without the well to sustain it. I had a feeling Fiorus knew it too, and that was why he hadn't already set to fixing things.

The cauldron suddenly pulsed with a bright flare of light, drawing all of our attention. Fiorus took a step toward it as the light flared again brighter than ever, then abruptly went out.

Several of the nymphs screamed. Aaliyah clutched my arm again. "What just happened?"

I shut my gaping jaw. The cauldron was now just inert metal. "I have absolutely no idea."

"Penelope," Lucas fumed. He stalked around the cauldron like he might kick it.

I dared a step toward him. "Who?"

"The devil." Before I could react, he had grabbed me again, tearing me away from Aaliyah. "Take me to Sebastian, now. If he is missing, she probably has him." He gripped my arms hard enough to bruise.

"I can't." I tried to pull away from him. "I'm only half celestial, what do you want from me?"

Magic surged through me, and I realized it was coming from him... *intentionally.* "Take me to him," he said through gritted teeth.

"You don't know what you're asking," I fought to speak beyond the overwhelming magic. "We could just as easily end up inside some dormant star. Or at the very least in a dumpster somewhere."

He pressed more magic into me. All the nymphs were watching us now instead of their ruined cauldron. Gray edged at the corners of my vision. If all of this magic didn't go somewhere else soon, I was going to pass out.

"Do you want to save him, or not?"

That was a loaded question if I had ever heard one. I could barely focus on Lucas' face as he asked it.

"Damn it all, fine." I shut my eyes, thinking of Sebastian's mocking expression. Then I thought of him kissing me, his hands roving across my body.

The entire world seemed to turn upside down, and all I could feel were Lucas' hands still gripping my arms. Then I felt heat. Who the hell had trapped us in a sauna?

Normally I wasn't great at sticking my landings, but Lucas kept me upright. He still gripped my arms as I opened my eyes.

We stood in a room made of deep red stone. The nearest window was stained glass depicting a strange celestial scene composed of planets I couldn't name. Through the colored glass I could vaguely see a vast rocky landscape.

Lucas released me, hissing like I had burned him. He looked around wildly, until his eyes focused on the other side of the room, on what I had already noticed.

Sebastian stood stiffly beside a beautiful woman with raven hair and his same uptilted eyes. She wore tight black pants, a white frilly shirt, and an honest-to-goodness frock coat with a black and white brocade pattern.

"*You*," Lucas growled.

The female devil curled one corner of her wide lips. "Yes, me." She held an old-fashioned lantern in one hand, glowing with the same blue light that had been in the cauldron.

To Sebastian's credit, he took a step away from her as he addressed me. "Eva, allow me to introduce my sister, Penelope."

23

"SISTER? You said you didn't know who she was!"

Sebastian tilted his head. "I said no such thing."

"Okay, but you acted like you didn't know her. You said you were going to do some digging."

His eyes flicked to Lucas, still fuming at everyone. "And I did just that. Unfortunately my digging led all the way to the hells."

My knees nearly buckled at his words. "Wait. Did you say the hells?"

"Well, one of them." The tone of Penelope's correction was far too similar to how Sebastian usually spoke to me. "And I must admit, you have saved me a lot of trouble. Here I thought I'd have to snatch you away myself."

I looked from her to Sebastian. "What exactly is going on?" Was he here willingly? Did he help her steal the nymph's magic?

"She is the one who claimed to know your mother," Lucas growled. "She had my feather. She must have stolen it."

Penelope's eyes flashed with fire. "My, such accusations."

"How did you get my feather?"

I looked at Sebastian as they spoke, but his expression gave me nothing. If anything, he looked bored. Was this it then? The ultimate betrayal?

But no... if he knew about his sister from the start, he wouldn't have bargained with Fiorus for the name.

"Why did you steal the nymphs' magic?" I asked before Penelope could taunt Lucas further.

She tilted her head. The similarities between brother and sister were almost eerie. "I stole it for you, dear Eva."

"I don't know what you're talking about." I looked at Sebastian. "Please feel free to step in and explain things at any time."

But it was Penelope who answered, "My little brother sees the superiority of my plan. Why spend so much time trying to nurture your magic, when I can just give you all you need?" She lifted the lantern, gesturing to it with her free hand.

"You want the bounty," I realized.

Her eyes sparkled at the very mention of it. "Everyone wants the bounty, Eva. But only I will succeed."

I took a step back, but there was nowhere to go. If

Sebastian wasn't on my side anymore— "I won't help you find my mother."

"Aw, that's cute, but I don't need your mother. I know who set the bounty. All I need to do is kill him for the blade." A smile slithered across her face. "And all I need is *you* to wield it."

"Yeah, I'm not going to do that either."

Her smile disappeared like it had never existed to begin with. "You will, or else my brother will break his contract with the goblin prince. The wild magic of the Bogs will run rampant. It will be rather fun to watch."

My gut clenched at her words. "You're lying. That contract can't just be broken."

She smiled again. "Oh my brother will lose his magic, of course. But I will make him do it. I would advise you not to test me on this."

There was finally a flicker of something in Sebastian's eyes, but I couldn't understand it. He lowered his chin like he was trying to tell me something.

"I don't think you can make him do anything," I said.

She laughed, an abrupt bark of sound that seemed to echo in the stone room. "I can and I will. I tricked him into a contract when he was just a child. He answers to *me*."

I looked at him again, but he didn't confirm or deny it.

"I tire of this." I had almost forgotten Lucas was standing right behind me, which was bad. He was exactly the type to stick a knife in your back. He stepped around me, pointing a finger at Penelope. "You ordered me to kill on your behalf."

She chuckled. "Yes, and I dare say you enjoyed it."

"But then you ordered me to protect *her*."

Penelope glided toward him. He didn't back up. If it were me, I would've backed up. But he stood his ground as she came to stand directly in front of him, having to crane her neck to meet his eyes. "Of course I did. Because with her, I have no need of her mother. I can use Eva to wield the blade."

"Why do you need me at all?" It probably wasn't wise to ask, since I had a feeling I was only alive because she found me useful, but I just had to know.

"The Realm Breaker was created by the sacrifice of your ancestors. Only one of your bloodline can wield it. The one who holds the blade now has no intention of giving it up. He just wants someone to find your mother so he can use it." She turned away from Lucas to approach me, making me regret speaking. "He thinks you're dead. We all thought you were dead. But here you are."

I shook my head. "None of this makes any sense."

Penelope glanced back at Sebastian. "Do you have to explain *everything* to her? How can you stand it?"

One corner of Sebastian's lips ticked up. "It has indeed been an *interesting* experience."

While her head was turned, I observed the glowing blue lantern in her hand. I needed to find some way to get it back to the nymphs to restore their well. Penelope thought she was going to use it to power me up, but I didn't need it. Lucas had proven that my four guys weren't the only ones that could give me a charge.

I glanced over at him. His rage had settled, and now his expression was calculating. I would have given a lot to know what he was thinking, because though we greatly disliked each other, we were currently in this thing together.

Only, he wouldn't care about the well. He only cared about revenge. He couldn't stand that Penelope had tricked him. And if my mom really had possessed one of his feathers, how had Penelope gotten it?

I realized she was watching me. "You should learn to school your expression, little celestial. Perhaps I'll even teach you, if there's time. But for now, you must make your choice. Do as I say, and your goblin prince can continue his little love affair with the Bogs. It will kill him eventually, but if you resist," she lowered her chin, catching a hint of the blue light from the lantern on her skin, "it will kill him far sooner."

I looked past her at Sebastian, who gave me a graceful shrug. Did that mean she could really do it? She could force Sebastian to break his contract, therefore losing his magic? I would have thought he would be a lot more upset at the prospect, but then again, he was great at hiding his emotions.

"I'll think about helping you." I pointed down at the lantern. "But only if you return that to the nymphs."

Penelope's nostrils flared like she was scenting my fear. "You are in no position to bargain, and I went to a great deal of trouble to obtain this."

"What trick did you put in Fiorus' contract? What did he miss?" It had to be something for her to so easily steal the magic.

"Oh, it wasn't him." She wiggled her shoulders a little and lifted her chin, seeming extremely pleased with herself. "It was those who opposed him. We made a deal that I would lend them the power to move the well. In exchange, I could call in a favor of my choice at any time."

"And your favor was them *giving* you their magic?"

"Well in my head, the favor specifically stated that I could touch the well. That's all I actually needed. Normally, only the nymphs can touch it."

In my opinion she was splitting hairs. The contract had been vague at best, but... it had obviously worked for her.

Now to somehow un-work it.

"Enough of this." Lucas stepped around me. "How did you get my feather from Helena?"

I froze at the name, something tickling the edge of my memory. I blinked at a flash of an image, my mother holding my hand when I was little. My father speaking to her, and he had called her... Helena.

But that wasn't the name either of us had remembered. And now she was being called Celeste. Just how many names did my mother possess?

Penelope smirked, and I realized something else. I recognized her. I had met her before. As soon as the realization hit, everything flooded back. I had been here before. When I was just a little girl, my mother had taken me to the hells.

That would have been after she severed the paths to the other realms with the Realm Breaker, but the hells were a near realm. A full-blooded celestial would have no problem reaching them. Hell, even I had been able to reach them.

But that meant...

Penelope's eyes shifted as my thoughts played out across my face. There was only one reason to visit a devil in the hells.

"You had a contract with my mother."

Her parted lips showed a brief moment of genuine surprise, but she recovered quickly. "And here I thought she had stolen all your memories."

I looked at Sebastian as I said, "Memories can't be stolen. Only hidden." He'd been the one to tell me as much. He had also admitted to knowing my mother far in the past, but he hadn't mentioned any contract with his sister, and that would've been far more recent.

"Did you know?" I asked.

He just stared at me blankly.

"You son of a—"

Penelope's finger whipped up, pointing at my face. "Now don't go insulting our mother."

I gritted my teeth. I still didn't fully understand

what was going on, but Penelope had a contract with my mother, and Sebastian never told me about it. "What did my mother want from you?"

Her eyes danced. Lucas was looming over her like he might pummel her, but she didn't seem worried. She gave him a small smile as she answered, "She wanted information on the ones hunting her, and she gave me a favor from an angelic in return."

Lucas seethed at her words. "It does not work like that. I only owe my oath where it was willingly given."

She tilted her head, draping that long dark hair across the shoulder of her frock coat. "Oh, dear, but it *did* work like that. I knew as long as I had the feather and I knew where it came from, I could get you to do whatever I wanted. And you *did*."

"And now you'll pay."

Sebastian was suddenly there pulling me aside as Lucas' wings flared out. He whipped them in a blinding arc toward Penelope, but his entire body froze mid motion. Only one toe still touched the ground. The only thing that moved was his throat bobbing as he swallowed.

"Unwise to attack a devil in the hells," Penelope tsked. Whatever she had done, she hadn't even broken a sweat. The lantern still dangled from one hand, undisturbed.

Sebastian gave me a meaningful look at her words, but I simply glared back at him. He had lied to me. I didn't care *what* he wanted me to know now. It was probably just more lies.

He gave me an impatient look, rolling his eyes toward his sister as she sliced her hand through the air, and Lucas fell to the ground in a heap. She stood over the fallen angelic, smiling. "Now, what am I to do with you? I am grateful that you brought Eva here, but she would have come for my brother eventually, so it's not as if you've done me any grand favor."

My eyes darted toward Sebastian again. So he was the bait to lure me here? And *why* wasn't he saying anything?

Lucas scooted away from her, then hobbled to his feet. Whatever magic she'd used on him had done more than hold him in place. He looked like he could barely stand. He clenched his hands into fists, but didn't attack again. It was shocking seeing him so easily bested. Even Sebastian had struggled against him.

But that had been on earth, where even Crispin's magic was weakened.

I looked at Sebastian again, my eyes wide as I realized what he had been trying to tell me. Devils were more powerful in the hells, where their magic flowed freely. For some reason Sebastian was being useless, but Penelope... she might not be quite so scary if we weren't in her domain. Only, I would need a boost to get us back.

I just hoped what I was about to do wouldn't get Mistral killed.

24

Sebastian didn't fight me as I dove into his arms and pressed my lips against his. In fact, he embraced me, his tongue sliding into my mouth, his hands kneading the flesh of my ass. I could see lights beyond my closed eyes, but I focused all I could on my connection with Sebastian, building our power together. I knew we wouldn't have long, and we would only have one chance.

I melded against his body and thought of Gabriel, knowing he would still be out in the city looking for me.

"I don't think so." I could feel Penelope's dark magic, so similar to Sebastian's, swelling as she drew near.

I cracked my eye open just enough to see as Sebastian removed one hand from my ass, and used it to grab his sister's wrist. Realizing what was happening, Lucas dove toward us, and that was the last thing I saw as everything seemed to turn upside down again. I could feel that golden cord between me and Sebastian, tying us together more than groping hands and hungry mouths ever could.

He kept me upright as we landed back in the park amongst the nymphs. Gabriel and Crispin were there, arguing with Fiorus. Even Seraphina had returned.

Lucas staggered away from Penelope, leaving her standing on her own as Sebastian pulled me tightly against him.

"Hey, I'm still pissed at you," I hissed.

He didn't let go, and instead lowered his lips to my ear. "She tricked me into a contract when we were young, that I must do whatever she says. But it is only valid in the hells."

My eyes widened in realization. That's why he had just stood there, and what he was trying to tell me about attacking a devil in the hells.

"You still lied about your sister," I grumbled.

He loosened his grip slightly, but didn't let go. "We will discuss that later."

"You!" Fiorus marched toward Penelope, who still had the glowing blue lantern in her hand, glowing brightly in the darkness.

All the nymphs seemed to recognize it for what it was. They closed in around her as the ground began to quake with their combined power.

Crispin and Gabriel joined us as Sebastian backed me away toward the tall iron fence surrounding the park. Ringo had been granted a spot on Gabriel's shoulder, and looked rather proud to be there.

Crispin moved to my other side, then turned to watch the show. "Gabriel about had a heart attack when the connection between us stretched within an inch of its life."

"I did not." Gabriel stood a few steps ahead of us, like he would intercept anyone who tried to come near.

Only there wasn't any need, not at the moment. The nymphs all closed around Penelope, and if I wasn't mistaken, all the trees had moved closer too. Water in a small decorative pond bubbled and swelled out of its boundary. I didn't see Lucas anywhere, so maybe he had put survival above his anger and hightailed it out of the park.

We move further away, pressing our backs against the fence. Part of me wondered if we should run, but I couldn't look away. At the center of the chaos, there was an explosion of blue light. It swelled outward, launching into the night sky in a blinding flash before pouring back into the empty cauldron.

The nymphs cheered, all gathered so closely together I couldn't see what had happened to Penelope.

"They won't have killed her, unfortunately," Sebastian said tersely, his arm still around my waist.

"She's the reason you can't return to the hells," I realized. "It's not that you don't have enough power to return there."

"It's both," he said, and if he minded that Crispin

and Gabriel could overhear, he didn't show it. Maybe he knew I would just tell them anyway. "When I realized she would be after the nymphs' well, I tried to summon her to earth, but she pulled me to the hells instead." He shook his head, his eyes drifting toward the celebrating nymphs. "She is much stronger than she used to be. I was forced to leave because of her, but the longer I was here, my magic dimmed. I needed enough power to travel back, and to destroy her."

"And the Realm Breaker would give you both."

He glanced down at me. "Not if it's true that only you can wield it. I was unaware of that information." Suddenly he seemed so unsure, something I *never* expected from him. I had a feeling being around his sister had actually shaken him.

"Trust me, if I get the opportunity to cut her down with a magical sword, I'm taking it. But only after she tells us who created the bounty."

"I'm not sure she actually knows. She is a talented liar."

"Not that this isn't fascinating," Crispin interrupted, "but we have the nymphs' attention again."

He was right, Fiorus had broken away from the crowd to approach us, and Seraphina of all people was walking by his side.

He gave his daughter a hesitant look as he reached us, then he addressed me. "I cannot believe you went to the hells to retrieve our magic."

I forced a smile. I probably shouldn't tell him that it

wasn't exactly intentional. "It wasn't right for her to steal it from you. That contract definitely wouldn't have held up in court. Not that it could ever actually go to court, but you get what I mean."

Fiorus' furrowed brow said that maybe he didn't, but regardless, he continued, "I had no idea how many of my own people were against me. How many wanted to come out into the world." He glanced back toward the glowing cauldron, most of his people now gathered around it. "And now there is no choice."

"We could still try to move it back to your realm," I offered weakly.

"The other realm is gone," Seraphina explained. "Only the well sustained it."

"So what will you do now?" Crispin asked.

Fiorus' eyes lifted to the raw iron fence behind us. It surrounded the entire park. The gates were closed in the evening, keeping humans out. "We will claim this land. Create our own boundary, as the others wish. Our well will give us enough power to do so."

"Um, you can't just steal a park."

Fiorus' eyes darkened. "Would you care to stop me? Once the boundary is formed, only nymphs and ones like yourself will be able to cross it."

He had a point. "Well I don't *personally* care if you steal the park."

He gave me a sharp nod. "Good." He looked at Seraphina. "Say your thanks. You will be needed for the ritual ahead." He turned and walked toward his people and their well.

Once he was gone, I lowered my voice. "Does that mean your exile is lifted?"

Seraphina smirked. "Having half his followers turned against him has rattled him. He now sees the value in his daughters." She shook her head. "But I won't be coming back. I like my life, and now I will be able to see my sister whenever I please."

"I'm happy for you."

She looked at each of us. "But what about you? The bounty on your mother?"

I winced. "You heard about that, huh?"

"Word travels fast." The guys shifted as she reached out and grabbed my arm. "You have helped my family. If you need help in return, I am here."

"After what you guys just did to Penelope, I may just take you up on that."

She smiled. "You do that." She looked at each of the guys again. "It has been... interesting, but we must start work on the boundary now. I would suggest those of you without celestial blood not be in the park when the ritual completes."

"Fine by me," Crispin said. "I have a princess to pick up from a vampire bar. I'm sure her werewolf escort is ready to be relieved."

Seraphina lifted a brow, but didn't ask questions. She simply turned and walked away.

"Let's get out of here," I suggested. "We have a lot to discuss."

)⋅⚬⚬⚬⚬⚬⚬((

CRISPIN LEFT us to pick up Elena, which put me alone with Gabriel and Sebastian at the steps to my apartment.

"I would require a moment alone with Eva." Sebastian's eyes were on Gabriel, daring him to argue.

But the goblin said nothing. He simply took my keys and went ahead of us toward the apartment with Ringo on his shoulder.

Exhausted, I sat on the steps. We were somewhere in the early hours of morning where the city was almost entirely quiet. I wrapped my arms around myself, shivering slightly. It had been a long night.

Sebastian sat beside me. "You jumped realms tonight. Twice."

I wasn't sure why, but the idea made me uneasy. "Only because I had you to lead me in one direction, and Gabriel to lead me back."

"Still. It's progress." He looked at me, his eyes shining in the darkness. "You regained one of your memories. What was it?"

"You really expect me to believe you didn't know your sister had a contract with my mother?"

"I knew your mother long before you were born,

and I have avoided my sister just as long. As you have learned, I cannot return to the hells while she is there."

"Then why did you try to summon her?"

He sighed. "I thought I could tempt her with information. Outwit her. I was mistaken."

"I'm surprised you're admitting it."

He gave me a strange look, like he didn't quite recognize me. "You saved me tonight."

"It was more complicated than that. If I didn't save you, Penelope could have used you to harm Mistral."

He laughed, his eyes drifting to the dark sky above. "True."

I looked at him, like *really* looked at him. There was much more to him than I understood—more than I would *ever* understand with how secretive he was. "Why did you really form your contract with Mistral? He believes you wanted him to die so you could access the wild magic of the Bogs. Gain enough power to go home."

He lowered his chin, that stubborn look flitting across his face.

"Hey, I saved you tonight. You said it yourself. And I know he didn't give you anything in exchange. You did it for free. Why?"

He was silent for a moment, then asked, "Did he tell you that I knew his mother?"

"We never discussed it, though I assumed you must have at least known of her."

"It was she who summoned me for a contract, unbeknownst to Mistral. We met at the gates, and she told me she was going to die. She paid the price for the contract she knew her son would request. She thought, if he would already bear the burden of the land, he should not pay dearly for it."

My pulse raced. Mistral still didn't know any of this. Surely he would have told me if he did. "And what did she give you?"

He simply smiled at me.

I gaped at him. "You can't just tell me all of that then not tell me what she gave you."

"The terms of every contract are private."

"But she's dead!"

His eyes danced with amusement.

"You are such an asshole." I started to stand, but he grabbed my wrist.

"You know it's no longer safe for you to stay here." He didn't say it like it was a question.

"We don't know that."

"Too many know of the bounty, and now with my sister involved, you are not safe."

"She's not as strong outside the hells."

"Neither am I." He stood, still holding my wrist, and a glimmer of magic flared between us.

I swallowed the lump in my throat. I hated this. I hated being chased from my home. "Where am I supposed to go?" I thought about the Bogs, but it would be difficult to make it to Emerald Heights to work with

Crispin. And now that I had realm jumped, we could finally progress.

"My apartment. It is well hidden, and it is neutral ground. Crispin and Gabriel can both access it."

"But not Mistral," I countered.

"And neither Crispin nor I can enter the Bogs."

He was right. There was no perfect answer, and whatever this was, we were all in it together. "Fine."

He lifted an eyebrow.

"What? I *can* be reasonable."

"You could have fooled me."

He had stepped closer, his dark magic tickling down my skin like a lover's caress. His hand lifted, stroking a light line across my jaw, lifting my chin, guiding me closer.

And gods curse me, I went willingly.

I thought he was going to kiss me, but instead his lips grazed my cheek, settling near my ear. "It is in my nature to read intentions. Hidden desires. Tonight, you weren't just saving Mistral."

I went still at his words, hating that he was right. Even after all he had put me through, I never would have left him down there with his sister.

"I will remember it." His words were barely above a whisper.

I tried to glare at him as he pulled away, but I knew I didn't quite manage it. I knew I couldn't keep what I was feeling entirely out of my expression. And what I was feeling was the overwhelming need to press my body against his. To feel that golden cord between us plucked like a harp string.

"I will wait while you pack your things."

Suddenly, the spell was broken. "You expect me to go tonight!"

He smiled. "You did already agree, Eva."

With a huff and a final glare, I marched past him up the stairs. All I wanted was a hot shower and my bed. I wanted to feel comfortable and safe.

And even though his apartment was probably as close to safe as I was going to get, comfort was not something to be asked of devils.

Because just as Mistral's mother had known, there was always a price.

25

"ARE you sure you want me to go?" Braxton sat next to me on the sofa in Sebastian's hidden apartment. Soft morning light cut across his tired features. None of us had gotten much sleep.

"Unless you want to hide out with us here." I pet Ringo, curled up in my lap. Unlike the rest of us, he was unwilling to give up his rest. His soft snores echoed around the silent apartment.

Braxton wrinkled his nose, glancing around. "Yeah, don't really like the idea of sleeping somewhere that Sebastian has free rein." His brow twitched. "Although you don't really seem to mind it."

I shrugged. "Silk sheets and a full bath."

"And a devil walking around in his underwear."

I snorted. "Absolutely not."

Braxton leaned back against the sofa cushions. A packed suitcase rested near his feet. It hadn't been easy to convince him to go, not only because he wanted to watch my back, but because, well, he was a big tough werewolf. They weren't used to running and hiding.

But I had already gotten him kidnapped by vampires, and I had brought crazed fairies into were-wolf lands. He knew I wasn't just being overly cautious in asking him to leave our apartment for a while. If Penelope got hold of him...

I shuddered to think what she would do.

I heard the door opening downstairs, and knew it must be Sebastian. Even if someone knew where it was, like Gabriel, they had to be let in.

Except I saw blond hair instead of black hair as someone came up the stairs.

Crispin tossed down a large brown leather suitcase, then straightened as he took in the apartment. "Not bad. Could use a few plants."

"What the hell do you think you're doing?" My eyes moved from him to Sebastian as the other man appeared at the top of the stairs.

Sebastian walked past him into the kitchen. "If I have to watch over you all the time, it will prevent me from finding information we sorely need. And Gabriel cannot be here at all times either."

Crispin grinned. "And I've got nothing better to do."

My jaw fell open. I looked in the direction of the single bedroom, then back at Crispin.

Only he didn't seem to notice my silent question.

He walked over to the sofa, plopping down between me and Braxton. "Plus, this will give us much more time to practice. Now that you have figured out how to jump to a near realm, I'm excited to see what else you can do."

I still seemed to be having trouble shutting my gaping jaw. "And King Francis is okay with this?"

"Oh he prefers it. Keeps us away from his precious daughter." He lowered his voice conspiratorially. "He found out about her bartending last night."

Oh gods, by the time we were through, I was going to have an elf king as an enemy. "Did she at least learn anything good?"

He smiled, pleased with himself. "Only that Elizabeta would like to meet you."

And there was my jaw hanging open yet again. "The master of all vampires in the city wants to meet me? Why?"

He shrugged. "It's all quite mysterious. She is allied with our king and has therefore honored his protection of you, so it's probably safe."

Sebastian walked around the kitchen counter, approaching us with a fresh cup of coffee in hand. "Elizabeta is nearly as old as I am, and bored out of her mind. She's probably just curious."

"And how old are you?"

He simply smiled.

"When you're ready to see her, Lilith will take you," Crispin continued.

Braxton's hanging jaw matched mine. "You're actually going to go meet her? After everything that happened with the vampires?"

"Elizabeta killed Ivan for his insolence." Sebastian took another slow sip of his coffee.

"So you're just going to trust her?" Braxton's voice was starting to go low and growly, and I realized we were probably near the full moon. Usually I kept track, but what could I say? Life had been chaos lately.

"She could have information that might help us," Crispin answered. "And if something goes wrong, Eva will just give one of us a kiss and we'll pop right out of there."

I glared at him.

He lifted his hands in mock surrender. "Hey, I didn't say it had to be me."

Braxton sighed and shook his head at all of us. "I can't believe I'm actually going to leave you all to your own devices."

Crispin patted him on the shoulder. "Don't fret, my friend. We have Elena to be our voice of reason."

Braxton glowered. "Yeah, not comforting."

Sebastian watched it all with an air of amusement, making me suspicious of why he seemed so pleased with everything. Of course, he was getting his way. I was hiding out in his apartment and would continue working on my realm jumping so I could find my mom.

We now knew she wasn't the one who had ordered Lucas to kill night runners—she probably didn't even know about it. And she might not even know about me.

As far as we knew, the glamour some fae had placed upon me still held, making my mom believe I was dead.

Unfortunately, that left us with more questions, not less. We still didn't know who was after her, or if the sword really could only be used by someone of my bloodline. Sebastian warned me I couldn't trust anything Penelope had said, but had admitted that it was all at least worth consideration.

For what good it did us.

For now, I could realm jump, but only if I knew someone on the other end. That would prove problematic since Sebastian couldn't go any further than the hells, even when I amplified his energy. It was a problem we would have to figure out soon, because I couldn't just hide in an apartment forever.

Sebastian was watching me like he could read my thoughts. He smiled at me, and I had no idea what the smile meant.

If only *I* could read *his* thoughts.

But that wasn't really in my wheelhouse. I would have to leave the mind reading to devils, and the forging of new paths to me.

Gods help us all.

Epilogue

I STOOD in the kitchen with Sebastian, drinking a cup of coffee with delicious, delicious cream. The cream had been my addition, and was currently the only thing in the fancy refrigerator. He set his cup on the counter, sliding it across the white marble away from the edge. Today he wore a black shirt rolled up to his elbows. When he wore darker colors, it was apparent that his hair was actually perfectly black, no hint of any brown or highlights.

He watched me with his usual calm expression. "Don't forget your promise."

I lowered my coffee cup. "Yeah, yeah." I had agreed to stay in the apartment for the day. Just a promise, no contract. I had been shocked he actually believed me, but maybe he knew that him believing me would make me actually do it. "But you better come back and tell me the second you learn anything from the fae."

He couldn't actually go into the Crystal Vale, but there were other parts of the city frequented by the fae. Our next order of business was to find out who had cast the glamour to hide me from my mother. To aim a glamour at a certain person, they would need to actually know that person, which meant they knew my mom. It was as good a lead as any, beyond hopping around to every near realm in search of her.

That would be our next task, once I figured out how to travel somewhere without one of the guys being on the other end.

He continued watching me.

"Crispin will be here," I huffed. "I'm not going anywhere."

The elf in question had gone out for food. We would be spending the day practicing magic, and maybe watching a few movies.

Hey, it was going to be a long day being stuck inside. Might as well make the most of it.

"We should talk about the connection binding us."

My eyebrows lifted at his words, because he had been avoiding all discussion of it since we got to the apartment. I had a sneaking suspicion being magically connected to someone made him uncomfortable.

And now it was making *me* uncomfortable, what with him watching me so intensely. "I don't know what it is. Just that it's getting stronger." I forced myself to meet his eyes.

He had moved closer, and now took the coffee cup from my hands to set on the smooth marble counter.

"What are you—"

His hands went to my waist, pulling me forcefully against him. I gasped, my spine betraying me as it arched for him. The magic was already kicking up between us, casting a red and purple glow on the white marble countertop.

His lips pressed against mine, assertive and hungry. I groaned against his mouth, and I could feel my veins turning molten with inner light as he gripped my hips and hoisted me onto the countertop.

And then he was back against me, my jeans-clad legs open around him. He fed at my mouth, one hand sliding up my thigh until he hit the middle seam of my jeans. His thumb slid lower, applying pressure and almost making me orgasm right then and there.

Some small little voice in the back of my head told me I was being an absolute idiot, but the golden cord between us seemed to pulse. I knew if I opened my eyes I would just see the purple and red lights, but with them closed, I felt like I could see the cord too, binding us together.

His thumb rubbed against me as he slowly leaned me back across the counter. He abruptly moved his opposite hand gripping my hip to pull me firmly against him. Feeling him hard through our pants, a trickle of reality settled in. This was going to happen, right now, on Sebastian's kitchen counter.

He leaned over me, sliding one hand behind my neck to pull me up for another kiss. His lips were scalding against mine, claiming me in every way.

He pulled away enough to meet my eyes. "Do you want this?"

The question was so unlike him, I didn't know what to say.

But my stunned silence seemed to be enough for him. His dark magic pulsed over my skin, lifting my shirt lightly enough for the fabric to tickle. I squirmed as I lifted my arms, the motion pressing him more firmly between my legs, making my breath hitch.

Once my shirt was gone, he looked down at me like I was a delectable feast before him, just as his magic found the clasp on my bra. It came loose and slipped from my chest, prompting Sebastian to use his hands to remove the straps from my arms.

He tossed the bra away with one hand, stroking his other on the inside of my wrist before lacing his long fingers with mine.

He pinned my hand to the counter, pressing himself over me as the other smoothed across my breast. His lips hovered just over mine. "Do you want this?"

My body was on fire with his touch, that golden cord pulsing, tugging things lower. It was all I could do to nod my head.

The next thing I knew I was up off the counter, my hands pinned over my head against the wall. His dark magic snaked across my abdomen, then the button on my jeans popped open. It was like he was working with extra unseen hands as they pulled the jeans down from my hips until I had to step out of them. I lost the under-wear at the same time, leaving me completely nude while he pinned me entirely dressed.

It should have made me feel vulnerable, but the way he watched me...

He dropped to his knees, releasing my wrists only to snag them with his magic instead, keeping me pinned. His fingers slid between my thighs, splaying them to make room. Just when I felt like my body was going to burst if he didn't put his mouth on me soon, he smiled, watching me with his hands between my thighs.

"You never really answered me, Eva."

I let out a stifled groan, squirming with my hands pinned and my thighs pressed open by his hands.

Still watching me, he pressed a light kiss to my inner thigh.

I gasped, my body thrumming with need.

Another light kiss, then his tongue darted out to taste my skin.

My eyes nearly rolled back in my head. "Yes, I want this."

"Are you sure?"

I let out another strangled groan. "Yes... please—"

.   .   .

He dove between my legs, his tongue and mouth hungry. I cried out, my knees buckling as he gripped my thighs and swung my legs over his shoulders, relieving some of the weight from my pinned wrists.

Our shared magic kicked up again, swirling around us, almost as bright as the light I was seeing behind my eyes as I neared orgasm. Just when I was about to go over the edge he stood, his pants already unbuttoned, his hard length pressing against me.

"Say it one more time," he demanded.

His length slid against me, so close to where I wanted it. I rocked my hips forward, sliding against him. So close.

"Eva," he breathed, his voice now strained with his own desire.

"I want this." I said again.

He slid into me, and stars bloomed behind my eyes. I pressed my shoulders against the wall, moving my hips against him. Then his magic was pinning me again. He pulled out slowly, then thrust into me with force.

"Oh gods, yes."

The words were all he needed to start pounding into me, rebuilding the orgasm into something even more spectacular.

He took me against the wall, right there in the middle of his sunny kitchen, with the city skyline looming outside the window. I cried out as he came, my own orgasm spilling over.

And suddenly I was in complete darkness, someone

pounding at the bedroom door. Just like Sebastian had been pounding me against the wall.

Holy hells. A dream. It was just a dream.

But I couldn't seem to communicate that to my quaking thighs as another light knock sounded at my door.

Silk sheets slithered across my skin, pooling between my bare legs, sending another shiver between my thighs. Even though Crispin was sleeping on the couch, I had gone to sleep in modest shorts and an over-sized T-shirt, both of which were now bunched up around me from tossing and turning.

Yeah, just tossing and turning. That's totally all I was doing.

Suddenly in a terrible mood, I threw back the covers and climbed out of bed. Ringo was still fast asleep on his pillow, snoring softly.

I walked toward the door, knowing it either had to be Crispin or Sebastian, though why one of them would wake me in the middle of the night was anyone's guess. Unless something bad had happened?

I picked up my pace, then opened the door.

Crispin stood outside with a lamp illuminating him from behind, shadowing part of his face. His blond hair was mussed, and he wore pajama bottoms and no shirt. I found my eyes catching on his bare chest. He was more like Mistral, muscled but lean, whereas Sebastian was a little taller with broader shoulders.

Oh gods—I really didn't need to be thinking about Sebastian's body right now. What was wrong with me?

I focused my attention back on Crispin. On his *face*. "What's wrong?"

He seemed almost a little embarrassed. "I was going to ask you the same question. I heard groaning, and I felt—" he cut himself off. "I thought maybe you were sick—or something."

I hoped in the darkness my blush wouldn't show, but he seemed to pick up on it regardless as his expression changed. "Ah, I apologize for interrupting."

"You weren't interrupting anything!" I blurted. "I just had a strange dream."

And it wasn't the first time I had dreamed about Sebastian. That first time, I wondered if he had done some sort of magic just to mess with me, but this time... I didn't think it was the case. He had kissed me in real life on multiple occasions, and never tried to push it further.

Nope, *I* was the one having all of *those* thoughts.

Crispin's expression shifted again. He seemed almost worried.

"What is it?" I asked.

His brow crinkled further. "Do you mind if I try something?"

I narrowed my eyes. "Depends on what that something is."

"Can you please just trust me?"

I thought about it for a moment, then nodded, realizing that I did trust Crispin. He stepped closer, and I forced myself to remain still.

One of his hands went to my waist, gripping through my baggy shirt, and with me already all riled from my dream, warmth prickled between us instantly. He gently pulled me closer, and I stayed perfectly still as he lowered his lips to mine.

He kissed me, and I was overwhelmed with the scent of springtime. Fresh leaves, clear running water, a breeze scented with moisture.

When I didn't pull away, he deepened the kiss. My stomach did a little flip, like going down in a roller coaster, and suddenly his hands were beneath the edge of my shirt, touching my bare skin. Nothing terribly inappropriate, but his bare hands on me pulling me against him made my thoughts swim.

I broke the kiss, pulling back enough to look into his eyes, both of us panting. "Crispin—"

"The thread is still there. Not just between you and the others, but between the two of us too."

"I know," I breathed.

His hands were still on me, his fingers absentmindedly running across my bare back. He seemed to realize what he was doing and abruptly yanked them away. "I apologize. I just... wanted to test it."

I balled my hands into fists at my side, once again going very still. Because if I didn't do that, I was going to go to him. For the thousandth time, what the hell was wrong with me?

"And did you learn anything?"

He managed a small smile. "It means, dear Eva, that we are all in entirely over our heads."

I smiled back. He just had that effect on me. Even as I was resisting licking his chest. "Tell me about it."

Also by Sara C. Roethle

A Study in Shadows

Hunters of the Helius Order have a single mission—track vampires, and kill them. Lyssandra lived her life by this purpose, until the day a vampire saved her from certain death. Now she is unwillingly bonded to him, a secret that will see her executed if her order learns the truth.

When she finds Asher, she'll cut out his heart for tying her to him, even if it kills her too. But when a young girl is found dead, Lyssandra's mission is derailed. In the gaping hole where the girl's heart once was, lies a single red rose. Lyssandra has seen the signature before, left by the vampire who took her uncle's life.

Karpov is one of the ancients, and his death is the only one Lyssandra wants more than Asher's. Unfortunately, Karpov is also the only being—dead or undead—who holds the key to Asher's whereabouts. If Lyssandra ever wants to find him, she'll have to work with her uncle's murderer.

Asher's death could finally bring her peace, but can she accept it when it means leaving her uncle's killer alive? Or will she fall into her master's waiting arms, unable to fight the pull of the unbreakable bond between them . . .

Books in the series:

Tree of Ages

Finn doesn't know what—or who—uprooted her from her peaceful tree form, changing her into this clumsy, disconnected human body. All she knows is she is cold and alone until Àed, a kindly old conjurer, takes her in.

By the warmth of Àed's hearth fire, vague memories from her distant past flash across her mind, sparking a restless desire to find out who she is and what powerful magic held her in thrall for over a century.

As Finn takes to the road, she and Àed accumulate a ragtag band of traveling companions. Historians, scholars, thieves in disguise, and Iseult, a mercenary of few words whose silent stare seems to pierce through all of Finn's defenses.

The dangers encountered unleash a wild magic Finn never knew she possessed, but dark forces are gathering, hunting for Finn and the memories locked away in her mind. Before it's over, she will discover which poses the greater danger: the bounty on her head, or a memory that could cost her everything.

Books in the Series:
Tree of Ages
The Melted Sea
The Blood Forest
Queen of Wands
The Oaken Throne
Dawn of Magic: Forest of Embers
Dawn of Magic: Sea of Flames
Dawn of Magic: City of Ashes

The Moonstone Chronicles

The Empire rules with an iron fist. The Valeroot elves
have barely managed to survive, but at least they're not
Arthali witches like Elmerah. Her people were exiled
long ago. Just a child at the time, her only choice was to
flee her homeland, or remain among those who'd
betrayed their own kind. She was resigned to living out
her solitary life in a swamp until pirates kidnap her and
throw her in with their other captives, young women
destined to be sold into slavery.

With the help of an elven priestess, Elmerah teaches the
pirates what happens to men who cross Arthali witches,
but she's too late to avoid docking near the Capital.
While her only goal is to run far from the political
intrigue taking place within, she finds herself pulled
mercilessly into a plot to overthrow the Empire, and to
save the elven races from meeting a bloody end.

Elmerah will learn of a dark magical threat, and will have to face the thing she fears most: the duplicitous older sister she left behind, far from their home in Shadowmarsh.

Books in the series:
The Witch of Shadowmarsh
Curse of the Akkeri
The Elven Apostate
Empire of Demons
Legend of the Arthali
Gods of Twilight

Twilight Hollow Cozy Mysteries

An inept witch, a cozy town, and an old dark magic.

Welcome to Twilight Hollow, WA, a small forest town with three resident witches. Adelaide O'Shea runs the Toasty Bean, imbuing her coffee and tea with warm, cozy magic. When a black cat crosses her path, she worries her new pet might be unlucky, and her suspicions are confirmed when the next thing in her path is a dead man with her phone number in his pocket.

And the cops aren't the only ones breathing down her neck over it. There's an old, dark magic in town, and it has its sights set on Addy. With the help of her two witch sisters, a handsome detective, and a charming veterinarian, can Addy solve the murder and escape the darkness? Or will she and her new spooky pet have to turn tail and run?

Books in the Series:
Familiar Spirits
Catnip Cantrips
Tricky Treating
Feline Charm
Hideaway Hexes
Kitty Coven
Haunted Hijinks
Purrfect Crimes

The Thief's Apprentice

The clock ticks for London...

Liliana is trapped alone in the dark. Her father is dead, and London is very far away. If only she hadn't been locked up in her room, reading a book she wasn't allowed to read, she might have been able to stop her father's killer. Now he's lying dead in the next room, and there's nothing she can do to bring him back.

Arhyen is the self-declared finest thief in London. His mission was simple. Steal a journal from Fairfax Breckinridge, the greatest alchemist of the time. He hadn't expected to find Fairfax himself, with a dagger in his back. Nor had he expected the alchemist's automaton daughter, who claims to have a soul. Suddenly entrenched in a mystery too great to fully comprehend,

Arhyen and Liliana must rely on the help of a wayward detective, and a mysterious masked man, to piece together the clues laid before them. Will they uncover the true source of Liliana's soul in time, or will London plunge into a dark age of nefarious technology, where only the scientific will survive?

Books in the series:
Clockwork Alchemist
Clocks and Daggers
Under Clock and Key

The Will of Yggdrasil

The first time Maddy accidentally killed someone, she passed it off as a freak accident. The second time, a coincidence. But when she's kidnapped and taken to an underground realm where corpses reanimate on their own, she can no longer ignore her dark gift.

The first person she recognizes in this horrifying realm is her old social worker from the foster system, Sophie, but something's not right. She hasn't aged a day. And Sophie's brother, Alaric, has fangs and moves with liquid feline grace. A normal person would run screaming into the night, but there's something about Alaric that draws Maddy in.

Together, they must search for an elusive magical charm, a remnant of the gods themselves. Maddy doesn't know if she can trust Alaric with her life, but with the entire fate of humanity hanging in the balance, she has no choice.

Books in the series:
Fated
Fallen
Fury
Forged
Found

The Xoe Meyers Series

I am demon, hear me roar.

Xoe has a problem. Scratch that, she has many problems. Her best friend Lucy is romantically involved with a psychotic werewolf, her father might be a demon, and the cute new guy in her life is a vampire.

When Xoe's father shows up in town to help her develop her magic, it's too little too late. She's already started unintentionally setting things on fire, and he lost her trust a long time ago.

Everything spirals out of control as Xoe is drawn deeper into the secrets of the paranormal community. Unfortunately, her sharp tongue and quick wit won't be enough to save Lucy's life, and Xoe will have to embrace her fiery powers to burn her enemies, before her whole world goes up in flames.

★ ★ ★ ★ ★ **Take your sparkly vampire and your sensitive werewolf, and shove them!**

★ ★ ★ ★ ★ **Best sleepless night(s) ever.**

★ ★ ★ ★ ★ **Fun-filled adventure that you just have to keep reading until the very last page. It is un-put-downable.**

Books in the series:

Demon Moon
Accidental Ashes
Broken Beast
Demon Down
Forgotten Fires
Gone Ghost
Minor Magic
Minor Magics: The Demon Code
Minor Magics: Dark of Night

Made in United States
Troutdale, OR
01/02/2025

27480583R00192